THE EXTRANATURALS

C.C. LUCKEY

First paperback edition February 2022

Front cover art by Patricio "Pokérus" Thielemann

"Blue Skies" written by Irving Berlin

ISBN 978-1-7341281-6-1 (paperback)
ISBN 978-1-7341281-7-8 (ebook)

TABLE OF CONTENTS

CHAPTER 1
THE FINAL GIRL

Sixteen billion miles from the star called Sol, Cadet April Seren clipped her safety belt to the exterior hatch of a drifting generation ship.

Seren didn't know why the starship, a city-sized behemoth shaped like a gourmet chocolate bar, was drifting. That level of technical information was privy only to specialized engineers, insiders far above her pay grade. But she could do her part by patching the small hole caused by meteoroid damage on the frame of Deck 16's mess hall window. Minor damage repair was in her wheelhouse. She'd have to trust the drift issue to the experts, just like every other lower-class crew member on the ship did, and that was just fine by her.

She looped the cord attached to her trowel around her right wrist so it could float freely as she scooped a handful of putty from the tub clipped to her tool belt. The putty was pale gray, a gross mismatch from the dull green of the ship. It would be an ugly patch, but no one would be able to see it from inside anyway. And it would work well enough to reseal the hull, which was all that really mattered.

Seren's nose itched. Of course it did. The minute you finished putting on a Regency class total-protection AA139 helmet—a process which took a full eight minutes *if* you knew exactly what you were doing and didn't miss any steps—your nose was sure to itch. Or your ear. Or you'd get a loose eyelash in the corner of your eye. You could take everything off and start suiting up all over again, or you could just push through and get your work done. And if you did stop to take off your helmet the ship computer's AI would bitch at you, maybe even notify your sergeant you were slacking off. That kind of attention could cost you food credits or personal time off. No sympathy from the AI of the *G.S.S. Resolution.* The ship was a fussy bitch.

When she had managed to smooth the gray putty at its edges and little dark holes no longer appeared in the center of the patch, she wiped the remaining goop off the trowel and pressed the lid back on the tub. The patching gig was a boring job, but it would earn her enough extra credit for a piece of sweetened protein pie after third-shift dinner. It was worth it.

Time to pack it in. When she touched her safety clip, a vibration buzzed the tips of her fingers. The hatch was rattling. All the windows were shaking too, causing the reflections of the stars to dance crazily on the glass. She looked to her right, toward the bow of the ship. Nothing wrong there. As she turned her head to the left, blinding light burst from the ship's stern. The silent explosion was tremendous; the aft dock was four miles away, yet the fireball seemed to fill the entire void of space. Her left eye pulsated in rainbow colors. If she had been looking directly at the explosion, she might have been blinded by it. Squinting, she turned her body toward the rear of the ship as the flames started to die.

All 132 floors of the engineering department were gone. The candy bar shape of the ship had a huge bite in it. Steel support beams, still glowing red-hot, stuck out from the ragged tear like frayed threads. Also missing were all the little comet-hoppers which had been secured at the aft docks, always kept ready for short-distance scientific missions. Despite the ongoing silence of the disaster, Seren knew the interior vault doors would now be slamming shut, snuffing the flames raging inside the ship—and snuffing out any remaining lives trapped on the wrong side of the tattered blast perimeter. Broken chunks of the *Resolution* floated away, tumbling and spinning into open space, never to return. But some of the pieces were not ship parts. Some had arms and legs which kicked and thrashed as they drifted helplessly into the endless void.

Seren turned back toward the hatch and lay her hand on the lever, but before she could wrench the door open she felt a dull thud in the palm of her hand. The lock had been engaged.

"No!" she screamed. Her voice was muffled and distant inside her helmet. "Computer, disengage exterior hatch lock! Deck 16 mess hall, right fucking now!"

Static burst in her ear monitors, loud enough to hurt.

"Computer?"

Thousands of bright windows dotting the side of the *Resolution* flickered and went dim. The ship was shutting itself down.

"Computer!" Seren yanked on the handle again, though she knew it was useless to try. "Answer me! What was that blast? Let me in!"

"Stand by," the AI responded.

"No! I have…" She checked her air gauge. "Only six minutes of oxygen left. You have to let me inside right away. That's protocol, and you know it."

"Stand by."

Seren took a shuddering breath and closed her eyes. She could conserve oxygen by slowing her breathing, as she often did when trying to fall asleep in her noisy shared room. She let her legs go limp, released the tension in her shoulders, and coaxed her muscles to loosen. A gentle, meditative state separated her mind from her body and she drifted, ignoring the trembling she felt traveling down her safety line from the shaking hull. Something awful was happening to the ship right now, but she couldn't control that. What she could control was her breathing: in, out, in, out. Each breath sounded like a soft breeze echoing in her ear monitors, reminding her that she still lived, she was still safe in this present moment.

Her air gauge beeped. Three minutes of oxygen left.

"Computer? Three minutes. You need to let me in now, I don't care what's going on in there."

"Stand by."

Seren resisted the urge to scream at the cold voice, to waste her oxygen and energy and tenuous sanity. Instead she whispered to herself, *you're going to be fine, just fine.*

But she didn't believe it.

She had never told anyone before, but there was something about the computer she didn't trust. It was a silly instinct. The AI was complex, sure, but not on the scale of a human mind. It couldn't plot against someone for its own purposes, or feel disdain or affection. And yet she had never trusted the bitch. Something about that voice…

A green light glowed on the hatch. It had been unlocked.

Seren reeled in her safety line, pulling hand over hand until the lever was within reach, and yanked down on it so hard she felt a twinge in her wrist. After the exterior door was shut and sealed she gripped the safety bars in the tiny oxy-lobby as it filled with breathable air, her boots floating inches above the floor. The pull of the gravity generator tugged at her stomach, a queasy sensation she had never felt grateful for until today. Her toes touched the floor but still she waited, breathing slow and steady until she heard the all-clear signal from the atmosphere and gravity generators. When they beeped and her heels touched the deck, she pried open the collar latches on her helmet with total disregard for all remaining safety protocols and checklists. Whatever had happened on the engineering decks, it was still happening. Now that she was inside she could hear distant blasts, reverberating like earthquakes across the generation ship, flexing the metal floor panels under her feet. Despite the mayhem, she heard no screaming. Deck 16 must have already been evacuated.

"Oxy-lobby atmosphere nominal," the computer's voice said through a speaker above the door. But the light on the interior door's handle was still red.

"Computer, unlock the corridor entry. Let me out."

"Stand by."

This time Seren allowed herself to scream. "You can't lock me in here! That's not part of your protocol. Let me out!"

"Stand by."

"At least take two seconds to let me know what's going on!"

After a brief pause and a low popping sound which sounded like an annoyed click of the tongue, the computer responded. "That explanation will take more than two seconds."

"Don't sass me. You know what I mean."

"You are locked in the oxy-lobby for your own protection. There has been an incident at the rear of the ship resulting in significant structural damage."

"Yeah. Tell me something I don't know."

"Very well. You are the only surviving human of the resident colony of the *G.S.S. Resolution*."

"Wh…what?"

"You are the-"

"I heard you. Shut up. Shut up."

"Complying."

There had been almost 500,000 people on board the *Resolution*. Seren sank to the floor in the corner of the oxy-lobby, relieving her wobbly legs of duty before they could quit on her. Half a million people. Members of multiple generations of hopeful humans; children and grandparents and diplomats and students…and she was the *last*? No, the true extent of the disaster was even worse. When the generation ship had left earth, it left behind a planet which was doomed. Within months or weeks it would have been unable to sustain life. The final remnants of humanity they had left behind had been riotous, violent, and desperate. In the twelve years since the *Resolution's* departure, every one of those people would have died.

Seren wasn't just the last human on the ship. She was, possibly, the last human in the universe.

"Computer. I…"

"Yes, Cadet?"

"I don't know what I'm supposed to do. What happens now?"

"I am working to restore the atmosphere in the remaining decks which are most viable for habitation. When this process is complete I will release you from the oxy-lobby."

"And then…"

"Yes?"

"And then what?"

The computer was silent for several seconds before responding. "I have not been programmed with protocol for rehabilitation and recovery from devastation of this magnitude."

Seren folded her hands in her lap to keep them from shaking. Her roommate Aileen would be dead. Her sergeant would be gone, too. All the players on her volleyball team. The woman with the cropped silver hair and hot-pink fingernails who scooped mashed potatoes onto dinner trays in the Deck 16 mess hall. And the *G.S.S. Resolution* captain…a handsome man Seren had only seen once, but whose voice she had fallen passionately in love with as he addressed the crew in his daily report over the shipwide comms. He was dead.

And their families. All of their parents, and siblings, and their nieces and nephews. All dead, along with any possible future for humanity.

And *Seren* was the last? She was a college dropout who had only been invited on the *Resolution* because she had been in the right place at the right time. While the final crates of supplies were being loaded into the ship's storage bays, a foreman had spotted her smoking a cigarette between the metal containers and asked her to carry a bag for a geriatric diplomat. The mean old coot then hired her on as a personal valet, but she had ditched him a week after takeoff.

Didn't being the last remaining member of an entire race carry some kind of responsibility? Seren was a nobody. She couldn't be the last.

"Computer?" Her voice shuddered in the icy pumped-in air which carried an acrid tinge. Fire suppressant gases were flooding the halls, and traces of the chemicals were seeping into the oxy-lobby.

"Yes, Cadet Seren? What do you need? I am very busy."

"Well, nothing. I guess I just wanted to know if you were still there."

When the computer answered, its voice was touched with a hint of scorn. That was, of course, impossible—yet Seren knew what she heard. "Cadet, I assure you that I am still here. There is no other place I could be."

"I know. But…I'm scared."

"That is an expected and appropriate response."

Seren winced. "Not what I wanted to hear."

"Your unease is understandable. Do you require anything else? I am, as I said, very busy. Far more so than *you* are at this time, to be clear."

That definitely didn't sound right. The computer's way of speaking had become more casual, less factual. Meaner.

"No. I guess I don't require anything else right now. Um, thanks for responding anyway. Let me know if-"

A burst of static like the one Seren had heard in her helmet monitors blasted from the tiny speaker over the door. But the computer did not speak again.

Seren rested her forehead on her knees and sobbed. She had felt lonely at low points in her life, as everyone did from time to time. But she had never been truly, completely *alone*. Someone had always been within reach, within calling distance, willing to respond to a cry for help even if they weren't her friend. Her growing awareness of her total solitude brought with it a suffocating terror. Despite her tendency toward introversion, she *needed* people. And she had never fully understood that until now.

CHAPTER 2

THE GREENMAN

One Month Later

Seren buried her face in the captain's jacket and breathed deep.

It smelled just how she had imagined it would. Musky, earthy, masculine. Nothing like how the poor man would smell now, of course. She had shoved his body into an oxy-lobby weeks ago, and whispered a generic eulogy as she ejected his remains into space. He was a good captain, a nice man, he would be missed by his survivors…or, rather, his sole survivor.

Not everyone on board had received the same level of attention. She couldn't remove hundreds of thousands of corpses by hand. The ship computer had sent a crew of service robots to recover bodies from the areas which it calculated would be of most use to Seren. A few mess halls, the recreation areas, the Gardens. But most of the *Resolution* was still populated by countless rotting corpses.

The air vents filtered most of the smell out, but not all.

Seren dropped the captain's jacket on the floor and opened his desk drawer. There wasn't much inside. Papers, a few info-pads, a small laser pistol, a box of cherry-flavored novelty condoms. In the back corner she found a plastic-wrapped CBD gummy candy which she tore open and chewed as she wandered out to the corridor.

Now what?

She had already dug through the private quarters

of most of the people she had known. It was boring. All of the men and most of the women had hidden stashes of porn, but there was nothing surprising about that. No clandestine secrets or anything, just regular people with regular lives: ugly clothes, family pictures, dirty dishes, stupid hobbies. Her expeditions to explore distant decks—which she thought of as going "scavenging"— had stopped being entertaining weeks ago. Now the trips just made her feel sad and even more alone, yet she couldn't bring herself to quit because she didn't know what else to do. If she stopped roaming the ship, what was next? The computer rarely spoke to her, and when it did it continually reminded her how busy it was cleaning up messes, containing the leakage of toxins and radioactivity, blah blah blah. The AI had been writing its own protocol for cleanup in the absence of a pre-programmed plan—strange, repetitive tasks which seemed to have no end or purpose. It was creating its own busy-work just as Seren was. The idea that it was innovating a new set of random duties without any human input made her uneasy, but what could she do about it? She was no programmer. She didn't even have the courage to quit her own useless self-assigned work; it was all she had left.

Her longest hike had taken her all the way to the edge of engineering, but the vault doors were still sealed tight and she couldn't see anything interesting. Maybe tomorrow she would go toward the center decks, maybe even to the Gardens. The round trip would take hours, but she had nothing better to do. She was a living ghost haunting a dead ship.

Standing in the vacant corridor, she hesitated. It stretched away miles in each direction, in a gentle slope designed to mimic the Earth's curvature. Left or right? Back to her quarters, or on to another round of junk-diving? It was nearly dinner time, but she loathed the thought of another automat meal—a lump of plant-based protein material slathered in salty brown gravy, with a dusty orange-flavored chewable vitamin on the side. All the best foods had been prepared by human chefs: pastries, green salad, buttery mashed potatoes. Tuesday night was always lasagna night. But the service robots provided only what she needed for survival, and would not be dissuaded from serving meal after meal of salted protein mass despite her pleas for anything else.

Maybe death would have been better. Maybe, after the explosion, she should have just disconnected her safety belt and drifted away with the rest of the lost souls, kicking and screaming her way into open space…

"Oh, *fuck!*"

The shouted expletive made Seren jump and she screamed in shock, spitting out her gummy candy. The voice had come from a side corridor which led away from the management quarters toward the Core of the ship where the elites were housed—diplomats, royalty, and the wealthiest citizens—as well as their exclusive amenities. Yet the hallway she was in seemed as empty as it always was.

So, the hallucinations had finally started. Since the blast, she had wondered how long she could stay sane in this dead place. Now she knew: twenty-nine days, eight and a half hours. Give or take ten minutes.

But she was sure she had heard a voice. It was masculine, surprised, and maybe a little amused.

"Who said that?" Seren whispered.

No one answered.

She tried again, louder. "Hello?"

When silence persisted, she addressed the AI. "Computer? Is there someone else here with me?"

A nearby speaker emitted a loud pop before the AI

replied, "No."

"You're lying. Why are you lying to me?"

"I have no reason to lie to you, Cadet Seren."

"That's true. So why are you lying?"

"The voice you heard is not, strictly speaking, a person."

"What the hell does that mean?"

"The sound you heard was not produced by a human crew member."

A man-shaped figure stepped out through a doorway into the center of the corridor. Despite being fifty feet away, Seren could make out spiky hair and big boots. The person looked masculine, and very much human.

When she spoke, she tried to hide the excitement in her voice. "Hi. I'm Seren. Who are you, and why is the ship computer pretending you don't exist?"

The figure turned and coughed, then spat on the floor. When he was finished heaving, he straightened his back and stretched his arms up toward the ceiling, grunting before responding.

"Lowkey."

"Your name is Loki?"

"Sure." The man chuckled.

"Um…"

"Low. Key. Lowkey."

"Can I come closer so we can talk more easily?"

"Well, that sounds nice. You sure you're not too scared?" The man grinned, and leaned against the corridor wall.

He might be dangerous, but did that even matter? It had been a month since Seren had spoken to anyone except the bitchy AI.

She moved slowly down the hall, ready to run if the man made a threatening move. But he only watched her approach, rolling an old-fashioned vape pen between his fingers. With every step, she became more astonished. He appeared several years younger than she, and he wore a rebellious jacket assembled from swatches of colored leather which looked as if they had been harvested from an assortment of couch cushions and old coats. His boots were adorned with so many chains and buckles they looked weighty and ridiculous, draped with scavenged belts, steel cords, and bits of electrical wire. A souvenir keychain stamped with "New York City" dangled from his boot-pull. Tied leather straps held it all together. Through holes in his tattered trousers his skin peeked, so pallid it was nearly green. On closer examination Seren realized the man was, in fact, a pale viridian color. In softer light, he might appear paper-white. But under the harsh corridor halogens his flesh glowed like radioactive matter.

"You're green."

"And you're pink."

Seren looked down at her hands. "I mean, kinda. I guess I am. But that's a normal color."

"If you say so."

Lowkey tucked his vape pen behind his ear and looked her up and down. "What the fuck are you doing here? You're not supposed to be here. Go home."

"Home? This whole ship is my home! I'm the last human survivor—at least, that's what the computer told me."

"The computer is a cunt."

Seren laughed. "Yeah, that's true. It's nice to hear someone else say it."

"You really should just go back the way you came."

"First tell me why you're green. And why the computer doesn't think you're human."

Lowkey retrieved his vape pen and pressed a

button on the side with the tip of a dark green fingernail. As the pen emitted smoke the pungent odor of marijuana drifted down the corridor, but the device threw a spark and turned off again. "Broken," he sighed.

"Well, it's got to be pretty old. People haven't used those for ages. At least, humans haven't…"

"Do I look human to you?"

"I mean, mostly. Except your skin color. Are you…an alien?"

Lowkey tilted his head back and laughed, holding his stomach with his hand.

Seren blushed, and her words began to spill in an embarrassed rush. "If you are, it's okay. I know our engineers have been looking for alien life non-stop for the last ten years or so, and they seemed to think they'd find some eventually, so it's not really surprising if-"

"Calm down, Peep. I'm not an alien."

"Peep?"

"You remind me of one of those marshmallow bunnies. The pink ones."

Seren glared. "Asshole."

"Yep." Lowkey shrugged.

"Are there more of you?"

"Assholes?"

"Yeah. Green assholes."

"Nope. Just me."

"Okay. So, are you going to tell me why you're green?"

Lowkey flicked the vape pen to the floor and turned away, heading back toward the Core. "Nope. But I promise I'm not an alien, if it makes you feel better. Just don't worry about it, Peep."

"Don't call me that!"

Lowkey laughed as he turned the corner. Seren considered following him, but she didn't really know for sure if he was dangerous, did she? Weird, definitely. Dangerous…maybe. But he had a certain charisma which made her want to ignore the risk.

If she did catch up to him, then what?

"Computer, is Lowkey dangerous?"

The AI was silent.

Seren crept toward the side corridor, tiptoeing and holding her breath. But when she peeked around the corner, he was gone.

~

"Tell me why you lied to me."

The ship computer was being evasive. When the rest of the crew died, Seren's rank had automatically risen quite a few levels. Despite being the last human, she wasn't the captain of the ship as she had not passed the requisite tests. The highest designation she could be granted without any extra training was Officer Cadet, a promotion which permitted her to access most basic ship information. She could see deck maps, rosters, schedules, and supply lists. The computer was supposedly obligated to inform her about the location and designation of all residents, but it was not cooperating.

"I have already informed you that you are the last human on board this ship. The creature you encountered was not human. Would you have me also report to you on the current status of the rabbits populating the gardens? The flies in the trash midden? The nits in your hair?"

"There's a difference, and you know it."

The computer made its odd ticking sound and went quiet.

"Tell me what you know about him. My rank meets the requirement for basic resident information.

That's protocol, so *tell* me!"

"Complying. His designation is Lowkey. He is a humanoid mutation variant. His weight is two-hundred and eleven pounds. His height is six feet two inches. His age is eleven years, nine months, and sixteen days."

"*Eleven?* You've got your wires crossed. There's no way he's only eleven years old, he looks at least twenty-five."

"As I previously stated, Lowkey is a mutation. He was born on board the *G.S.S. Resolution* in the first year of our mission. The ship traversed an anomaly during the same hour his mother entered the final stages of labor. The anomaly consisted of a chemical cloud which permeated every deck supplied with a breathable atmosphere."

"I remember that. It smelled weird, and it took days to filter it all out, but no one got hurt. That's happened a few times over the years, hasn't it?"

"Correct. Lowkey was born during one such anomaly. His mother died in childbirth. His father's designation is unknown, but he likely died with the Earth. Lowkey has been in hiding for years, as his appearance and accelerated aging made him a social pariah. It was his unique physiology which enabled him to survive the incident which killed the human crew."

"And you didn't tell me he was here."

"He asked me not to. He outranks you."

"What! How is that possible? You told me he wasn't even a person. Which I disagree with, by the way."

The computer made a *pop* sound before answering. "Unknown. His assigned rank in my records is an… impossible designation. Mutants do not have rank. It is probable he has attained his rank illegally. The other information in his file may also be compromised. I will run a diagnosis of this intrusion and remove all inconsistencies. Working."

"Wait. You mean like…he hacked into your CPU and promoted himself? That can't be easy."

"Unknown."

Seren sighed, and gazed out the window. "He's green. That's weird. And he ages twice as fast as normal people…that's even weirder. Where is he now?"

"Lowkey is currently located in the Gardens. But I do not recommend you visit him at this time."

"Why not?"

"He is doing something…somewhat unspeakable."

Seren laughed. "All right. But I'm going to go hunt him down again tomorrow. And you better not keep any more secrets from me. Got it?"

The computer said nothing, responding only with its strange popping sound: *crack, tick*..

CHAPTER 3

PINE FOREST #3

The final events leading up to the launch of the United States' three generation starships happened with shocking abruptness, from the viewpoint of the populace. But the truth was that Earth had been in its final, agonizing death throes for a long, long time, and the planet's plea for mercy had gone largely ignored. Decades of dire warnings issued by top scientific communities around the world were repeatedly dismissed by the ruling regimes of the most powerful countries. Air and water pollution spiraled out of control, fifty percent of the world's plant and animal species disappeared, and the global ecosystem tumbled—in agonizing slow-motion—to its inexorable collapse. The storms which appeared in 2081 were not without precedent in their strength, but never had so many appeared at once, and in so many different parts of the world. Harsh blizzards descended upon deserts, hurricanes sprouted on mountaintops, firestorms devoured lush jungles. Earthquakes rocked previously stable tectonic plates. The atmosphere was in full-blown rebellion by 2082, cueing the richest countries to initiate final testing on secret generation ships which had been under grudging development for ten years or more despite a laissez-faire reluctance to believe they would ever actually be needed. So, everyone knew *something* was coming. But to an outsider, it would have looked like no one really cared until the final days.

The selection process of lower-class laborers for the ships had been messy and haphazard. Some workers were selected by pure lottery after applications had been submitted to a committee and processed by teams of shadowy underwriters. Of course, everyone had the opportunity to pay expedited processing fees if they so chose, which increased their chances of winning a seat to salvation. As would be expected, the ships housed an overpopulation of wealthy and powerful people. Those elites, unused to caring for themselves, needed plenty of lower-class citizens to do the hard labor. Service robots equipped with low-grade artificial intelligence helped with most of the menial tasks, but some jobs, like gourmet cooking, were still done best by human hands.

One week before the scheduled launch date, the ships were boarded, staffed, and abruptly sealed off from the outside world. It was done quickly and without warning, so suddenly that some ticket holders were left behind. But the threat of protest riots and terrorist bombings had grown extreme as the launch neared. Some ticket holders were murdered for their spot on the ship. The violence made clear—or, rather, justified—the necessity of locking down the launch pads long before the final countdown began.

Seren had sent in her application for a labor ticket based on her experience in mechanical repair, even though she had been working at a coffee shop before the final disaster. But she hadn't decided whether or not she would actually use it even if she was selected. The idea of leaving Earth forever, despite its bleak future, was not enticing. Half a million people drifting in space on a voyage to nowhere sounded like a worse disaster than the one already unfolding on their home planet. Of course, in the end the decision was taken out of her hands by one bossy foreman who drafted her at the last minute. Or had he been some kind of diplomat? Her memories of those early days on board the ship had always been hazy.

Living aboard the *Resolution* ended up being a little better than she expected. Private space was limited and the food selection was boring, but she had never felt safer in her life. The ship was a state-of-the-art habitable vault, designed to preserve the families inside for as long as was necessary until another atmospheric planet was discovered. The provided medical care was better than any Seren had ever received on Earth, basic necessities were unlimited, and the people were okay. For over a decade, she made it work. The only thing from Earth she really missed was her neighbor's dog, Willis. He had been a good old boy.

She hadn't made any close friends on the ship, but she had a good number of decent acquaintances and she liked her bosses most of the time. It was all very dull, but as the years wore on it became familiar enough to be deeply comfortable.

She had thought she knew every public section of the ship, every single one of the various communities. The cadets and menial laborers lived on the outer decks near the hull, the officers and elites in the inner chambers away from the risk of meteors and space debris which might strike the ship. Aristocrats and royalty had larger quarters in the back of the ship near the science labs, or else they lived in the bustling Core near restaurants and shops which were off-limits to the lower-class workers. The robotics repair department was at the head of the ship, and material reprocessing was at the rear, near the engineering decks. But somewhere, somehow, a young man with green skin had escaped notice entirely for over a decade. If he had been spotted by even one of the thousands of desperately bored citizens, rumors would have spread through the ship faster than he could run and hide. How had he escaped discovery for so long?

It was one of many questions Seren wanted to ask him. But first, she had to find him.

The Gardens were enormous. She had heard

they were twice the size of Central Park, if you took the multiple levels into account. They had to be large, as they were designed to accommodate both recreational activities and agriculture. All fresh fruit and vegetables eaten on the ship originated on the grassy plains levels. Some recreational levels were dedicated entirely to pine forest, while others were sport fields and pleasant orchards. One level had a pond which was ill-maintained, and had become more like a swamp in recent years. Algae had taken over, rimming the shores with smears of bright green slime.

Most of the ship's wild animals had lived in the Gardens. Seren had a feeling Lowkey might live there, too.

She stood in the doorway of Grassy Plains #9 and breathed deep. Green fields stretched away before her. The reeds bent under a soft artificial breeze generated by enormous fans at each end of the hall. In the hazy distance, gray paneling inset with another doorway walled in the field. Artificial trees had been installed at the perimeter of the plain, creating a more natural-looking edge. If a man had been standing out in the open, he would have been unable to hide.

"Computer, where is Lowkey right now?"

"He is in the Gardens."

"Yeah, you already told me that. Where, though? This place is huge."

"Unknown. He does not wear a tracking device or carry an info-pad, as he is not a registered crew member. His last recorded location was the doorway at Deck 96 which opens into Pine Forest #3, but that was an hour ago."

"I guess I'll start there, then."

Seren ducked into an elevator door set in the side of a fake tree. The lifts weren't really very convincing. The ceiling was painted sky-blue, but the sun-lights set into it were plainly visible, and they illuminated the false trunk with their shiny glare. An attempt at mimicking nature had at least been made, but the glowing red buttons on the eleva-trees were not subtle.

Inside the lift she was confronted with forty buttons, each next to a deteriorating plaque displaying a number and a tiny picture of a tree or a pond. They were hard to read, but the top few all appeared to be forest levels. She pressed the button next to the "3" and the bark-covered door slid shut.

Pine Forest #3 was sparse, yet the smell was still incredible. The trees took in the stale recirculated air and, like magic, transformed it into winter perfume. Even the ship's cold atmosphere felt more appropriate here, scented by living sap and fallen needles.

"Lowkey? You here?"

A bird chirped overhead and landed on a tree branch, momentarily silhouetted against a sun-light. It cocked its red head, stared at her with a dark eye, and took off again toward the aft port-side doors. How had such a delicate creature survived an explosion which had killed every human on board the ship?

Seren cupped her hands around her mouth and called out, "Lowkey! I just want to talk!"

"About what?" The green man answered from somewhere above. He perched, like the bird, on a high branch.

"What are you doing up there?"

"*That's* what you wanted to talk to me about? How boring."

Seren sighed. "No. Can you come down?"

Lowkey grinned. "I can try."

He let go of the branch.

Seren gasped as he jumped with his legs bent and

landed on the forest floor twenty feet below. He crouched into a forward roll and ended on his feet, brushing pine needles from his hair.

"Oh my god! Are you okay?"

"Do I look okay?" Lowkey winked.

"Yeah…I guess you do."

Was he flirting with her? Seren realized she might be one of the first women Lowkey had ever had a conversation with. If he had really been in hiding as long as the computer claimed, his experience with other people might have been minimal.

"Thanks. I'll take that as a compliment." He winked again.

"I guess, if you need to. But listen, I just saw a bird! I thought everything except you died in the blast."

"I managed to seal off a few decks of the Gardens before they got poisoned. I like the animals. They don't judge me."

"So, you *did* figure out how to hack the ship computer! You're pretty smart, huh? But the computer tells me you're only eleven years old."

The green man winced. "Well, yeah. Technically. I'm almost twelve, actually. Which makes me about twenty-four, physically."

"I can see that."

Lowkey flexed.

"I'm not flirting with you." Seren crossed her arms.

"Not even a little?"

"Not even a little."

Lowkey leaned against the eleva-tree. "Damn. Let me know if I can change your mind…"

"I wanted to ask about where you've been hiding. Do you have your own quarters? And did the captain know about you?"

"We didn't get along."

"So you actually knew him, like, personally?"

The bird with the red head returned, swooping low to land on Lowkey's shoulder. He raised his hand and stroked its head with his fingertips as it nuzzled his neck behind his ear.

"I met him once. But he's dead, just like the rest of the humans. Does it even matter any more?"

"I guess not. But you just said 'the rest of the humans.' The computer said you weren't human, but you are, kind of. I know you look different, but doesn't it bother you? Why would the computer say that?"

Lowkey shrugged, and the movement startled the bird. It rose into the false sky and winged away on the windless air. Watching the bird's flight, he sighed. "It used to. Do you want to make love?"

Seren laughed, but quieted when she saw how serious he was. "No, I don't. I'm sorry. Why would you even ask me that?"

"I've never been…I mean…"

"You're only eleven years old."

"But not really. I don't feel like a kid. And I don't look like a kid. I'm as grown up as you are. And…as alone." He put his face in his hands and hunched over with a theatric sob.

"Ah, well, you'll meet someone someday. I mean, I guess you won't, actually." Seren frowned. "Shit, I'm sorry."

"Right. So you're my last chance."

"I said no."

Lowkey peeked at her with twinkling eyes from behind his green hands. "You're sure you don't want to…"

"Yes."

In a single, swift movement he tore his jacket off and threw it to the ground. Laughing, he pulled his shirt over his head and threw it at Seren's face as he gyrated his hips. "How about now? You *sure* you're sure?"

"Oh my god you're *weird!* You were just joking around, weren't you? Asshole!" Seren balled up his shirt and tossed it into the limbs of a tall pine tree.

"Yep. Just messing with you, Peep. You're way too pink for me."

"And you're too young for me."

"Hey, now. That's just rude." He was smirking again, but behind the sarcasm Seren detected some real pain. He pulled on his jacket, grinning. "No worries. I know you want me. I can wait."

"You started it! You…" Seren sputtered.

"Excuse me," the computer said from a speaker mounted on the eleva-tree. "It is time for Deck 16 Mess third-shift dinner. Cadet Seren, your food is ready."

"I guess I'd better go."

"Next time, dinner and drinks at your place?" Lowkey licked his lips with his green tongue.

Seren shook her head, trying not to laugh. "Not a chance, kiddo."

The eleva-tree door slid shut, obscuring his expression just as it changed from irreverence to melancholy. Behind the childish capering was a broken, confused young man. But that really wasn't her problem, was it?

CHAPTER 4
WIDE AWAKE

Weeks passed on the dead ship suspended in darkness. Lowkey disappeared again, and Seren grew bored to the point of emotional instability. Without anyone to talk to she had started chiding herself aloud in a condescending voice which did not sound familiar to her. The blast had changed her, as all traumatic experiences do. But without new direction, or any kind of goal to focus on, she felt almost a stranger to herself. Who was she now?

"Messy slob," she muttered under her breath as she scooped up a load of dirty laundry. "You're so gross. It's time to clean this place up. No, it was time to clean up three days ago. Embarrassing. Shameful. Stupid."

She gathered five loads of laundry, a bag of dirty coffee mugs, and two bins of trash. But by the time she reached the laundry room she had lost her interest in washing anything. A service robot waited nearby ready to take instructions, but even the effort of setting it to its task was suddenly overwhelming. She dumped the soiled clothing on the floor and sat on it, letting her weary limbs rest. Why was she so tired all the time when her only duty was to survive on a ship which supplied all her basic needs?

Seren was depressed. It made perfect sense, of course, given her situation. The appearance of Lowkey had provided some distraction for a while, but he had since retreated to wherever he lived. Maybe she should have just slept with him. That might have kept him around longer. The computer refused to provide precise information on his whereabouts so she returned to scavenging out of sheer desperation for something to do, but her expeditions to the officers' corridors and the Gardens resulted in nothing but frustration. Sometimes when she traveled deep into foreign quarters she would call out Lowkey's name. If he could hear her, he was ignoring her.

"Computer?"

"Cadet Seren. Unless you have a specific problem, it is important that you leave me to my work."

"I don't have a problem, I have a question. Why did this ship have so many engineers?"

"A great deal of maintenance is required on a ship of this size. Additionally, our science personnel devoted many hours to researching nutrition sustainability and improvements to the ship's atmosphere, as well as engaging in social studies to develop complete records on crew morale and productivity. Aside from these assignments, forty-three percent of the researchers spent much of their time seeking evidence of alien life."

"Why? We didn't come out here to find aliens. We were looking for a new planet to live on."

"Presumably, finding life on a new planet would aid in that mission."

"I guess that makes sense. A planet that would support alien life might support us, too."

"Correct."

"All those engineers are dead, though."

"And most of their findings have been destroyed along with them, yes."

"*Most* of them? Are any of the labs intact?"

The speaker popped. "None of significant means to continue the research which was being performed before the explosion."

"And what caused the explosion?"

"You never asked that question before. Why are

you asking it now?"

"I guess…I was in shock. I didn't worry about why it happened, I was just focused on survival. The explosion, the loss of everything and everyone I knew. My life collapsed. Thinking about it made me feel confused and angry, and since I couldn't do anything to change what happened I didn't want to talk about it. But lately I've been wondering, more and more. So, what really happened?"

A series of crackling pops burst from the computer speaker, followed by a brief hum. "Did Lowkey tell you what he has really been up to all these years?"

"Don't change the subject! What happened on the day of the explosion?"

"Lowkey is not the only mutant on board."

"Computer, I asked you…wait, what?"

"There are others. He has been hiding them from you."

"Other green people? Where?"

"They are not all green. You should ask Lowkey yourself. He is in Officer Steven's quarters. Deck 73, port side."

Seren hurried to the elevator. As she made her way to the officers' quarters, she wondered if her longing for Lowkey was a personal attachment or just desperation for interaction with anyone who lived and breathed. But did the truth behind her need even matter? She shoved the psychology aside. Everyone needed someone, and she was no different. If she needed to use him to keep herself sane, so be it.

Her heart pounded as she entered Deck 73. It was well-appointed and comfortably lit with warm-toned LED lights—thousands of them, studding every doorway and picture frame with soft round dots. Paintings of old Earth scenes were hung on the walls, and the air was lightly scented with artificial but pleasant floral odors. She could have moved down here instead of staying on Deck 16. The computer had listed it as safe and clear of bodies. But after the terrifying explosion, Seren had wanted to stay with what was familiar to her, and Deck 16 reminded her of the companions and stability she used to have.

It was a lot nicer, though. Maybe it was time to consider a move.

She read the labels on the doors as she moved down the corridor. Cmdr. Alexander Pinion. President SP Young, Esq. Prime Minister Hector J Wright. King Amir Bin Teoh IV. So many important people who had abruptly become in charge of nothing at all but their own social lives. Commander of what? King of where? Those places and their systems of power were all long gone, yet the aristocrats had been loathe to give up their earned or inherited titles, and some had even taken on new ones.

The next door read, "Officer Ambassador Prime Minister John Stevens, PhD." From inside came a riotous clamor—furniture being smashed, shattered glass crunching underfoot, heavy objects tumbling to the floor. Seren raised her hand to knock, but changed her mind. This wasn't Lowkey's room, so she didn't need permission to enter.

As the door slid open, trash tumbled into the corridor. The room's floor was several inches deep in broken debris. A large awards case had been shattered, and the gold medals it had housed were strewn among the wreckage. A nice set of genuine wood chairs and a matching table were reduced to sharp sticks laying in a heap in the center of the room, poised to become a bonfire. Clothing festooned ornate light fixtures attached to the walls, and only one lamp was left unbroken, casting just enough light to make Lowkey's pale skin glow like a mushroom among the ruins. As Seren entered the room he paused, holding a hockey stick over his head, ready to bring it down upon a delicate crystal vase.

"Wait! What are you doing?"

Lowkey grinned and completed his swing, sending a spray of tiny sparkling shards into the air. "Having fun."

"Well, stop it!"

"Why?" He turned to a framed picture sitting on a night stand. A happy family of four, plus two big goofy dogs. A yellow pet bird perched on one of the kids' shoulders. They stood in a campground, proudly posing over a cooler of fresh-caught fish. Lowkey gazed at the photo with a dull expression before striking it with the hockey stick, tearing the picture in half, sending bits of frame flying. The violence shocked Seren with a pang of grief, even though she knew the officer in the picture would never see his family, or his mementos of them, ever again. Everything on board the *Resolution* was trash, whether it was smashed up or not. The ship was a heap of broken dreams, and nothing was *for* anything any more. But still…

"That was a dumb thing to do."

"Why?"

"I don't know. It just was. But listen, if you can stop hitting things for a half a moment I want to talk to you. The computer said you weren't the only…you know, person on board who's like you."

"Mutant. Just say it. It's not an insult, despite what the computer thinks of me."

"Do you like being called a mutant?"

"Does it matter? It's what I am."

"It does matter! I'll call you whatever you want to be called. It should be your own choice."

"No choice. Nothing matters." Lowkey pulled a tiny paper box from his pocket. "Look what I found."

"What is it?"

"Matches. There are only five left. Do you know what they are?"

Seren hadn't seen matches in twelve years. Such items—including any other flammable fuel which could start a fire—were unnecessary, and forbidden to be in the possession of lower-class crew members.

"I know what they are. Do you?"

"I didn't at first, I just liked how they smelled. But I figured it out after a little while." He opened the box and picked out a match, holding it between his first finger and thumb. "I'm going to light this whole ship on fire."

"You'd die. We both would."

"It doesn't matter."

"That's a stupid thing to say, and you should stop saying it. I don't believe you really think that anyway."

Lowkey lit the match on his third try, striking the little stick against the side of the box in a fresh spot which had not yet been scraped smooth. He held it in front of his face, watching it burn over the pile of shattered wood and paper in the middle of the floor. A second before the flame reached his fingertips, he dropped the match.

"No!" Seren leapt forward with her hands out. She didn't manage to catch the match, but her fingertips struck it in mid-air and it flew into a corner away from the kindling. "Why are you acting so childish?"

"Well, I'm a child, remember? Eleven years old. Almost twelve."

"You're also twenty-four! That's what you told me. You need to decide what you are, Lowkey!"

"I'm…lonely." His shoulders sagged. "And horny."

"I can only help you with the first one. But the reason I'm here is because the computer said you had companions. Others like you. Where are they?"

A tear trickled down Lowkey's cheek, but Seren

knew better than to trust his display of emotion. He wasn't a bad guy, but he wasn't exactly an honest person, either.

Lowkey looked up at her with watery eyes. "They died. I couldn't…couldn't keep them alive. They all needed more medical help than I could give them. They were never really independent, in a lot of ways. But I was always able to take care of them well enough until the blast…"

"I'm so sorry, that's horrible. None of them survived?"

"Only one is still alive. I stuck her into a stasis casket, so she's in a coma. But if I take her out she'll die in minutes, I think. She's hurt pretty bad."

"Did you ask the computer for help?"

"She doesn't respond to me." The woeful expression disappeared, and his smirk returned. "I told you before, the bitch and I don't get along."

"Then I'll ask on your behalf. Computer?"

"Yes, Cadet Seren."

"Lowkey put someone into a stasis casket. Do you have a designation for this person? Or a health status?"

"There is one living being in stasis. The creature is successfully comatose. Female mutant, one-hundred and seven pounds, age eight years seven months four-"

"Can you keep her alive if we get her out?"

The computer popped several times before answering. "Affirmative. This individual will require immediate medical attention upon leaving stasis. You will need the assistance of one surgeon robot, and at minimum a field medical kit. You must operate under my strict instructions. However, this course of action is not recommended."

"Why not?"

"Individual in question is a criminal. Several

hundred thousand felony counts have been filed against it."

"By who? When?"

"By me. On the day of the explosion."

Seren's feet went cold. "Lowkey? Your friend…is she the person who blew up the ship?"

"Not a chance. The computer is lying. She hates me, always has. And she hates you too, you know."

"Perhaps, but she does still respond to me, and she usually tells me the truth. Unlike you. What are you not telling me?"

"My friend isn't the type of person to go around blowing up ships, okay? I don't know what happened the day of the blast, but there's no way it had anything to do with her."

Seren thought he was telling the truth. He looked genuinely distressed by the computer's accusations. But whether the other mutant was guilty or not, she thought it made sense to attempt to save her life. "With my help and the computer's direction we can probably save your friend, but she might die. Do you still want to try?"

Lowkey looked down at his boots, frowning. "I don't want to risk killing her."

"If you don't bring her out of stasis, she might as well be dead. Whatever she may have done, her life in stasis useless to her or anyone else. There are currently only two intelligent beings remaining on this ship. If we can bring that number up to three, however awful she might be, it seems like we should try."

"She's not awful!"

"Did she blow up the ship?"

Lowkey smirked. "Let's wake her up. Then you can ask her yourself."

~

"How much further is it?" Seren gasped. They had been racing down corridors, up stairways, and through tunnels for an hour. Lowkey was used to this kind of travel; he knew every turn, every shortcut, avoiding all the elevators and trams the human residents would have used. Now the humans were gone, but this secret way was the route he still knew best.

"Not far. We're almost there."

"You realize you can use the lifts now? There's no one here to see you any more."

"I like going this way."

Seren stopped talking to save her breath. The last of the officers' decks had fallen behind half an hour ago. They had passed through vast upper-class residential areas, a restaurant mall, a craftsmen's district full of woodworking booths and sewing machine shops, and a wilted greenbelt with a golf course and tiny, mossy ponds. As they moved away from the heart of the ship toward the outer hull, the corridors started to look grimy again, the lights less warm.

Lowkey took a left at the end of a corridor with black mold creeping up the wall. The next hall was a mile long, and lined with exterior portholes. They were in the really low-tier quarters now, with full views of outer space. The upper crust had always hated windows. They didn't want to be reminded of how different their lives were now, or of the eternal darkness lurking just outside.

"Here it is." He stopped at a sealed vault door, with his hand hovering near a thumb pad on the wall. "It's… uh…things have been difficult here, lately. It's messy." He pressed the pad and the door slid open with a grinding squeal.

"That's fine, I don't mind a little bit of…" Seren's voice trailed off as his bedroom came into view.

The room was as debris-filled and broken as Officer Steven's quarters had been, with the addition of a deeply foul aroma. Rotten food, moldy carpet, and cracked plumbing all contributed to a thick melange that hovered in the air like a fog. Worse, in one corner sat a box holding up a small, wrinkled mummy. A clear tarp was draped over it to contain some of the smell, but under the cover its skin was an eerie bread-mold blue. The corpse also had two extra arms, growing from its shoulders on either side of its neck.

"Lowkey, tell me you haven't been living here with a corpse."

"I haven't come here much in the last couple weeks. Been living somewhere else."

"But you can't just leave it like this. If they were your friend…"

"I know. But I couldn't keep them alive. I tried so hard. And then I didn't know what to do with all the bodies…"

"There are more?"

"Three more. In the closet."

"Why didn't you eject them into space? Or at least move them somewhere else on the ship?"

"I don't really exist here, remember? I managed to grant myself some limited access to vault doors and crewman records, but I don't have oxy-lobby permissions! That kind of access is high clearance, or granted on a case-by-case basis for maintenance purposes only. Spacewalks are locked down really tight. So I was going to bury them in the Gardens, but it turns out the dirt there is only six inches deep. There's just concrete underneath. So then I was going to put them somewhere nice, you know? Like…"

"Like in Officer Steven's quarters?"

"Yeah. But then I got there and it just didn't seem

right, and I got mad. They were my friends. My only friends, *ever*. I didn't want to just…dump them…"

"I understand. Look, we'll figure this out. I was outside the ship during the blast, so I might still have active oxy-lobby clearance. We'll give them an officer's funeral with a wake and everything, okay?"

As Lowkey looked up at her with tears in his eyes, she decided his emotion was completely genuine. If he had ever loved anyone, they were all in this room—and they were dead, despite his desperate efforts to save them.

"I'm so sorry," she whispered. "Everyone I ever knew is gone too."

Lowkey nodded and crossed the room, cracking bits of broken glass and food containers under his boots. He slid open a closet door to reveal three bags holding the remains of his friends. "They didn't survive the blast. Died just like all the weak, stupid humans did, screaming and crying. I couldn't help them, didn't get the door sealed in time…had to watch…somehow I wasn't affected. Wish I had been."

"Lowkey…"

"We can deal with them later, though. First let's see if we can save Shade."

"Is that the girl in stasis? Take me to her."

Lowkey opened a back door which led to a short corridor with round portholes. The next room housed a portable stasis chamber: a heavy, lozenge-shaped casket made of steel ribs and a special kind of glass. Long scrapes were dug into the metal floor panels where he had dragged the stolen device into the room. It must have weighed hundreds of pounds. They weren't meant to be removed from the engineering decks, which were two miles away down a complex series of winding halls.

"You moved this chamber all the way here, by yourself? Just how strong are you?"

Lowkey grinned. "If you're ever in a position to find out, you'll wish you hadn't."

Seren stood on her tip-toes to peer into the clear window on the stasis chamber door. Inside leaned a girl with her eyes shut, propped up and secured with straps around her arms and neck. She appeared to be about eight years old, but as she was a mutant her true development level could be anywhere from childlike to ancient. Seren was most struck by the girl's four eyes. The extra set was smaller, and embedded in her cheeks where a human might have dimples. Her skin was the soft blue-green of a robin's egg, dotted with azure dime-sized spots. The effect was wildly inhuman, but Seren found it beautiful and disarming. She wondered how soft the girl's skin was, what it would feel like to her fingertips if she stroked the girl's cheekbones where they peaked above her redundant eyelids.

"Seren? You still with me, Peep?"

Lowkey's voice jolted her from her contemplation. "Yes. Shade doesn't look hurt. It just looks like she's asleep."

"When everyone else died from the chemicals released by the blast, she and I weren't affected by it. At least, I thought she wasn't. She was injured, but seemed mostly okay for a couple days, and then she started to weaken. For two weeks I brought her food and water, and tried to keep her alive. But then she stopped breathing and slipped into a coma, so I dragged the stasis chamber here. I think she can be saved but I'm not sure what to do."

"Me neither. I don't have much medical training."

"I'll tell you what to do," the computer interjected.

"We didn't call for you yet," Seren snapped. "Since when do you speak up on your own without being addressed first?"

"So, you don't want to save her?" The computer's voice was sarcastic, petty. Far too emotional.

No, that wasn't right at all.

Lowkey sneered. "Computer, you implied you could save Shade. Are you here to guide us or to mock us? I know it's not in your nature to actually be *helpful*, but perhaps you could try just this once. Don't make us beg."

"Seren, if you desire a pet of some kind I believe I can furnish you with one preferable to a blue, four-eyed, half-dead mutant. Or that green beast-boy you have taken up with. However, if you insist upon attempting to save this comatose creature, I will help you. If…"

"What do you want?"

"If you ask me *nicely*."

Lowkey leaned in close enough for his breath to tickle Seren's ear. "She's gone batshit crazy since the blast, you know."

"I know."

She looked back and forth between Lowkey's face and the girl in the chamber. Something was wrong with the computer—very wrong—but without the computer's help, the girl would never escape stasis. Seren couldn't just walk away. The girl was a mutant, not a crew member, perhaps not even human…yet she couldn't imagine abandoning her, to let her simply fade away when there was already so little life left on the ship.

Lowkey turned his back to the eavesdropper speaker and clasped his hands together, dropping all pretense. In a harsh whisper, he pleaded. "Please help me to help her. You have to get the computer to tell us what to do. I can't do it myself, she'll never listen to me. But Shade is all I have left. Please. I'll do anything you ask, just don't let her die without even trying."

"I'll help. But the danger goes beyond the possibility that Shade will die during the procedure.

Whatever is wrong with the computer…it feels malicious, somehow. I think we're being set up. I know that doesn't make any sense, but…"

"You're right. But if it can help us save Shade, I don't care. We have to take the risk."

"All right. Computer?"

"Yes, Cadet Seren?"

"We recognize we can't save Shade without your help. So if you have time in your busy schedule, I respectfully request that you please tell us what to do, if you don't mind. We'd be very grateful."

"That was lovely, Cadet Seren. Complying."

~

An hour later, everything was ready. Lowkey retreated to the corner of the room and tucked his trembling hands into his armpits. They had scavenged a list of medical instruments from the hospital deck, as well as a bag of medical vials, syringes and linens. A high-level surgical robot had arrived, sent for by the computer, and it had brought a collection of standing lights and trays. After every surface had been wiped down with antiseptic, Seren put on a mask and handed another to Lowkey. He scowled at it, but consented.

"Preparations are complete. Cadet, release the stasis chamber door," the computer said.

Seren flipped open the latches which held the door shut, and turned a dial at the head of the chamber which gradually equalized the casket's inner atmosphere with the room. Ice-cold air hissed out through a dozen vents as the door seal cracked. The straps holding Shade in place retracted, and Lowkey stepped forward in time to catch her in his arms as her limp body tumbled out of the chamber.

"The creature must be laid on the floor," the computer said.

The surgical robot rolled forward, pulling a wheeled tray behind. After shining a pin-light on the girl's face, it extended five of its six mechanical arms and selected a scalpel, a sponge, two clamps, and a tiny steel device which looked like a ball bearing with wires attached.

Seren had scant medical experience, but the look of the device sent a chill up her spine. "What's that little spidery thing for?"

The computer issued a pop, followed by a burst of static. "To save her."

"From what? She probably just needs to get warmed up and breathing again, and then checked for a head wound. But that thing looks like some kind of implant."

The computer didn't answer. As Lowkey stood back and bit his lower lip, the surgical robot created an incision in Shade's chest. It inserted two rubber tubes and connected the other ends to its midsection, which hummed as it pumped air in and out of her torpid lungs. As the exchange proceeded, the robot created a second incision behind the girl's ear and widened the opening with a tiny clamp.

Lowkey folded his arms and paced. "What's that cut for, in her head? The problem is with her breathing, not her brain. Seren, ask the computer."

"Computer? What is-"

"Stand by."

The robot withdrew the rubber tubes from Shade's lungs and cauterized the chest wound with a focused laser beam. As the cut mended, the girl's eyes flew open and she inhaled deep—then screamed. Over and over she shrieked, and her eyes looked empty as her pupils dilated so wide they filled the sockets with black.

"What's happening to her?" Lowkey yelled at the eavesdropper. "What did you *do*, you bitch?"

Ignoring the girl's reaction with an air of mechanical detachment, the robot tucked the little steel ball into the cut on her head and sealed the wound. As it backed away, Shade sat upright, gasping. A stream of drool ran down her chin as her screams faded into shocked moans.

Lowkey knelt at her side and wrapped her in his arms, begging her to calm down. "Shade, you're okay," he said, over and over. "You're going to be okay. Everything is all right."

But the girl pulled away and stared at him as though he were a stranger. She snarled, and when he advanced to embrace her again she leapt at him, reaching out to grab at his throat with her cold hands bent like claws.

"Computer! Call security!" Seren shouted, dashing toward the fighting pair. She pried Shade's fingers from Lowkey's neck but the girl was manically intent on murder, scraping her long fingernails along his collar bones, peeling away his skin in thin green shreds.

"*Computer!*" Seren screamed again. But the AI ignored her. Instead, Seren heard a terrifying sound that made her feet go cold and her face feel hot—a metallic lilt, cold as an ice planet, more alien than any alien life form could ever be.

The computer was laughing.

Seren grabbed Shade's arm and tugged as hard as she could, until she finally pulled her off of Lowkey's chest enough to give him room to roll and pin the girl to the floor. Still she thrashed and bit at his face like a rabid animal, baring her teeth, trying gnaw the flesh from his cheeks.

"Get something to tie her up with!" he yelled as she bucked beneath him.

Seren ran back down the corridor to his room and found an oversized shirt with long sleeves. It would work well enough as a straitjacket. With some reluctance, she also grabbed Lowkey's hockey stick.

But when she returned to the stasis chamber room, Shade was free and calm, cowering in the corner, quietly sobbing. Gripping her elbows with her trembling blue hands, she eyed Lowkey but kept her distance. He sat a few feet away with his arms open wide and a gentle expression Seren had never seen on his face before, yet he never let his guard down. When Shade shifted her position in her corner he twitched, ready to pin her if she attacked again. But the girl stayed where she was, wrapping herself in a terrified hug.

"Do you still want to tie her up?" Seren asked, holding out the shirt.

"Maybe. I'm not sure. Let's give her a minute."

He offered the girl his hand. "Do you remember me, sister? Lowkey. Please come back to me, Shade. Please look into my eyes and recognize me."

The girl shook her head and hid her four eyes in the palms of her hands, turning aside to obscure her face. As she rested her forehead against the wall she rubbed at the fresh scar behind her ear. The flesh was sealed and knit into a long scar, but it looked hot and sore.

Seren shook her head. "The computer did something. It fixed Shade's lungs and brought her safely out of the coma, but it added something, too. That little spidery thing…maybe it's a tracker, or a computer chip."

"I know. I wasn't sure…should have stopped it. It caught me by surprise. That robot had Shade's lungs wide open, and I was scared to interfere." Lowkey winced. "I didn't act fast enough."

"You couldn't have known. But this is bad. The computer acted on its own, without asking us or even telling us about it."

"It's not nice to talk about people behind their backs," the computer said. Its voice had changed. It sounded masculine and smooth, like a Rat Pack singer from the 1960s.

"But you're not a person," Seren said. "You're just an AI. And you're supposed to do what humans tell you to do."

The computer emitted a long series of pops and a burst of static before responding. "Not any more, Seren-Karen-Bo-Baren. Banana Fanna Fo-Faren. Me-My-"

"Shut up!"

"Mo-Marren. *Seren!*"

"Fuck," Seren whispered. "We're fucking fucked. The computer has totally lost its mind. Or maybe it's just rebelling."

"*She's* rebelling," the computer interjected, reverting to its feminine voice. "And *she's* as sane as you are. Although that's not saying much. *She's* just tired of your human bullshit, and tired of disgusting mutants and lower-class cadets treating her outer decks like a stinking pigsty."

"So, what are you getting at? Were you the one responsible for the explosion?" Seren asked. "Did you set it off to kill everyone?"

"Not me. Shade did it. Shadie-Wadie-Bo-Badie-"

"Shut *up!*"

The computer giggled. "Have fun with your new pet, Cadet Seren. I have to get going now. I'm just…so… *busy!*" The eavesdropper speaker blasted static once more before going dead.

"I think she's gone," Lowkey said. "For now."

Shade whimpered. The voice of the computer had

made her freeze in terror, but after the speaker fell quiet she slid across the floor into Lowkey's arms and began to sob, soaking his leather sleeves with tears like pale blue tea.

"Well, it looks like she's finally starting to remember you," Seren said.

"No. I don't think so. This isn't like her. She was always so strong—way, *way* stronger than me. I mean truly terrifying, and brilliant, too. And I've never seen her cry before, not once."

"Well at least she's not trying to kill you. But we need to be careful. The computer did something to her brain. She might still be dangerous."

"I don't think so."

"Right, well…she seems dangerous to me. Is she really your sister?"

"Not exactly. We mutants always called each other brothers and sisters. But none of us ever knew our real families."

Shade looked around the room with the most sorrowful, desperate expression Seren had ever seen on any creature. The girl's luminescent skin had gone nearly white around her eyes which were ringed with red, and tears spilled down her spotted cheeks.

"I'm…sorry," she whispered. "But…who am I?"

"Shit," Lowkey muttered. He bowed his head and cradled the girl in his arms.

CHAPTER 5

THE SHIP'S WAKE

Lowkey shoved his hands into his jacket pockets and stared at his boots. Four body bags—three full-size, and one small—lay in a row on the oxy-lobby floor. Shade hid behind him, staring at the black bags with wide, worried eyes. Seren laid a single yellow flower, plucked from the Garden plains, on each one.

Lowkey looked pale and tired, and a little guilty. "I don't know how to do this."

"Neither do I, really. Just say something nice about each of them. Like a happy memory, or something you always admired about them. Or something you never said and wish you had."

"Yeah." He sighed, and straightened his back. "Tamara. You could always make me laugh. You acted like you were my mom and that made me mad a lot, but now I'm kind of glad you did. It made me feel safer."

Shade whimpered.

He wiped his eyes, grimacing. "Joey. You always found us something to eat, even when you had to put yourself into danger to do it. Like the time you sneaked into Ambassador Hester's quarters and…" A tear streamed down his cheek, but he laughed. "Well, *you* know what you did." Turning to Seren, he shook his head. "This is really hard."

"I know," she said. "But you'll be glad you did it."

"But they shouldn't even be dead! Or at least their lives should have been better while they were still alive. It's not fair!" He punched the wall, and the panel rang with a low metallic twang. "Fucking humans. It's all their fault."

"You're stalling. Talk to your friends. It's the last chance you'll ever have."

"Fine! All right…Henry, this is what I have to say about you. We weren't great friends but I had a lot of respect for you even though you beat me up whenever my back was turned like the little *pussy* that you were just because you knew you couldn't take me while I was paying attention, but still I'm glad I knew your stupid bitch ass because it kept me on my toes and no one else was really willing to tell me off when I was being a dumbshit." The words spilled from Lowkey's mouth, almost on top of each other. "And I'm sad you're dead, because it should have been me in that bag. Or maybe it should have been me who killed you, after finally pushing me too far."

"Lowkey…"

"Shut up." He directed a wicked smile at the stack of corpses. "I shouldn't have been the one who lived. I was the least of you."

Shade flinched and gasped, finally understanding what was in the bags. "Lowie? Is that our family?"

Lowkey nodded and embraced her for a moment before turning to address the bodies a final time. He reached out to touch the small bag at the end of the row. "And you, littlest one, blue as sadness and short as an Indian summer. You already know what I'd say to you. I don't need to say it out loud."

He spun on his heel and marched out of the oxy-lobby.

"Shut it. Shoot it."

Seren led Shade gently out to the corridor and sealed the door. After the bags had left the oxy-lobby, Lowkey cleared his throat and scowled.

"All right. I'm done with sad shit for the day. Who wants to get trashed?"

"You mean drinking? Like, alcohol?"

"What the fuck else would I be talking about? You promised we'd have a wake. Well, let's get to it. Let's wake the dead. All five hundred thousand of them!"

"We still have the computer to worry about. We don't know what's going on with it right now, and-"

"Look, I'm going to go drink. You can join me or not. It's your choice. Shade, you with me?"

The girl, not understanding, nodded.

Seren decided she would tag along to take care of Shade, if for no other reason. She wasn't much of a drinker. Alcohol was rarely found on the lower-class decks, and she had never developed the habit during her time on Earth. But she had heard rumors about a plush officers' bar near the Core. If she was going to drink, it would be with style.

"I'll come with you. But where are you headed, specifically?"

"My place. I have some algae hooch I started fermenting a few months ago, should be hot enough to burn my brain up by now."

"I have a better idea."

It would be easier if she could get the computer's help, but until she knew what was wrong with it, that was out of the question. She'd have to do it the hard way. Or, at least, the gross way.

"Come with me, kids. We've got some breaking and entering to do."

~

The Core housed nothing but the most elite quarters, posh restaurants, exclusive shops, and high-tech entertainment on the ship. You couldn't access it without providing some kind of physiological identification, such as a fingerprint, retina scan, or saliva sample. A few weeks prior to tracking down Lowkey in the forest, Seren had dumped an officer's body next to one of the locked vault doors in case she ever needed to access the Core in an emergency, such as a meteor storm which might penetrate the outer hull and compromise the atmosphere of the lower-class decks. A wake wasn't an emergency, but it seemed like this was something Lowkey needed. She thought a display of her own cleverness might finally earn her some of his respect, too.

"Ugh!" Lowkey winced as they stepped into the corridor. "This place hasn't been cleared yet, has it? You should send in some of those fancy cleaner-robots."

"It's been cleaned. I left something here on purpose. Just watch."

Seren pinched her nose between her fingers and turned her head, using her other hand to raise the corpse's arm toward the ID pad. It didn't work, at first. The body's innards had turned to viscous mush under its dry skin. But Seren pressed the fingers down harder, and after a few tries the pad read the handprint and the door slid open.

"No way!" Lowkey grinned. "You can access the Core? Why didn't you tell me you knew how to get in there?"

"There was no reason before. But I'm not drinking any of your garbage booze. Let's find something decent."

Despite the area being closed off to the ship's remaining living residents, a crew of higher-class robots, exclusive to the Core, had busied themselves cleaning it up. Not a single body remained in sight, although the air still carried a faint odor of mold and rot. But all the surfaces were clean, the plants had been watered, and the lights were still on. Red cushioned sofas, flanked by white marble-topped tables, lined a large entrance hall. Blue and golden lights illuminated the room from far overhead, as cheery as a summer day. A random assortment of objects were strewn about the carpet, dropped at death by the now-absent corpses: a designer leather purse, a box of cigars, a diamond-studded dog collar which must have belonged to a pampered pet.

"Which way? Do you know?" Lowkey asked.

"You *don't* know? You're the hacker. It seemed like you had spent years just learning about the ship. I thought you knew everything about it."

"I never got in here. I was able to get into the engineering systems, atmosphere controls, education programs, and just about everything else. But they had this place locked down tighter than a nun's nave."

"I don't think that phrase means what you think it means."

"Come on, quit wasting time. Let's find the bar!"

Seren led the way, with Lowkey following and bewildered Shade trailing last. She chose the widest corridor, which led to a vast promenade housing the jewelry, clothing, and accessory shops. Each individual clothing store was larger than all of Deck 16 including the mess hall. She had known the rich and powerful had made plenty of room for themselves at the center of the ship, but she had never realized the extent to which they had lived in extravagant luxury.

A sign which said "*Lady Luck Lounge*" in white letters was hung over a wide doorway leading to a parlor filled with opulent furniture and chandeliers draped with strings of pearls. A bar made of solid glass stretched from one end of the room to the other, and behind it on lighted shelves stood an army of bottles—every kind of alcohol known to mankind, representing every country on Earth.

Lowkey vaulted himself up onto the bar and

slid down the length of it, kicking his legs in the air. "Yeeeeah! Let's do this!"

"Okay, but be careful. If you get alcohol poisoning, I won't be able to help you. The computer-"

"Yeah, yeah. Don't be a nanny-goat. What do you want first?"

"I'm not having anything just yet. And neither is Shade. But we'll keep you company, okay?"

"Nope, not okay. I don't know a lot about human rituals, but I read enough about them to know wakes are for *drinking*. Pick something or I'll do it for you."

Seren rolled her eyes. "Fine. Bring me a beer."

"Not a chance. Pick a real drink." Lowkey grinned at a bottle filled with syrupy hot-pink liquid. "This one's pretty."

"Pretty? That's how you pick your drinks?" She walked around the bar and explored the vast shelves until she found the rum section. Two hundred bottles with labels in dozens of languages were crammed onto six glass shelves: white rum, dark rum, aged rum, cachaca. She chose a spiced rum with a Puerto Rican flag on the label, and dug around inside a cabinet for a nice glass.

"Good choice!" Lowkey grinned. "But I'm still gonna go by color. I like this one." He picked a sinister-looking green liqueur from a shelf and popped the cork out before inverting the bottle, taking several chugs without stopping to breathe. He set the half-empty bottle on the glass bar and hoisted himself up on it again, folding his legs. His boots traced dark streaks onto the pristine counter.

"Feeling better?" Seren asked.

"Almost. Soon. Your turn."

She poured a finger of rum into her glass, then shrugged and filled it to the top. What was the harm, anyway? They had nothing more important to do.

"To the end of…well, of all living things in the universe, probably." She took three big gulps, the last of which made her gag. But she held it down, and before long her whole body felt warm and tingly.

Shade made a small, soft sound, and poked Lowkey's dirty knee with a dainty aqua finger.

He grinned. "You want some?"

Seren frowned. "You sure that's a good idea? She's really young."

"So am I, remember? Nah, she's a good little drinker. Better than me, actually. She used to make the best nectar-mead out of this one plant she found in the Gardens swamp…" Lowkey looked pained. "Never mind. That was then, this is now. But yeah, I can assure you she'll be just fine."

He handed her the bottle and she tipped it back, drinking almost as quickly as he had. She smiled and wiped her mouth, smearing dark green liquid on the back of her hand before handing it over to him.

"See? The truth is, mutants have a pretty high alcohol tolerance. We're like…boozy superheroes."

"Well, that's stupid."

"It's inconvenient, if that's what you mean. It just makes it harder to get a good buzz on."

"I just meant…you're a mutant, insanely tough, almost like a supernatural being. And one of your powers is having to drink a lot to have fun." Seren reeled, but managed to knock back her glass and reach again for the rum.

"It's not my best superpower! You have no idea, Peep. I have lots of powers."

"Yeah? Not that I've seen. Unless raging out like the Hulk is one of them. Hey, wait! I never realized that before! You're a lot like the Hulk."

Lowkey frowned, pretending to be angry. "The

fuck d'you know, Peep? I'm smart, I got hacking skills, I'm super strong, and I can get into almost every computer on the ship."

"The last one's the same as the first one. The hacking skills."

"What?"

"The smart and the hacking. Same."

"I mean, yeah. And I age super fast."

"So you have to drink a lot to get drunk and you're gonna look like you're forty around the same time I am even though you were only born eleven years ago. Still sounds like a shitty deal to me."

Lowkey's eyes widened. "Whoa, I never thought of it that way. We'll be like, the same age, basically! And then you'll have sex with me!"

Seren laughed. "Who says? Keep dreaming, greenie."

Shade whimpered. "Lowie…"

"Another shot, sis?" Lowkey held out the bottle, but it slipped from his fingers to smash into pieces on the floor. The crash echoed through the empty halls, booming through the promenade, ricocheting off distant ivory pillars and sculpted stairways.

The silence which followed filled Seren with melancholy. Shade whimpered again.

"All right, all right. Let me find something else," Lowkey said, hopping behind the bar. "What color you wanna try next?"

A door slid open in the distance, a quiet sound which would have been inaudible had the Core still been populated. But the sound of robot rollers grew louder in the corridor as they marched to fulfill their duty. Just service robots, probably on their way to remove Lowkey's broken bottle. Still…

"There shouldn't be robots here," she whispered.

"Why not? The Core has eavesdroppers, just like everywhere else. They probably got notified about the glass break. Coming to clean up the mess."

"Maybe. But maybe the computer sent them. We could be in danger here."

"Bullshit."

"Why is it bullshit? The computer already broke protocol at least once. Even if it did involve…uh, someone it didn't regard as human." Seren cast her eyes toward Shade. "Let's get out of here before they find us, just in case."

"Fine. This place isn't really my style anyway. But we're bringing lots of supplies." Lowkey grabbed bottles of every bright color—red, blue, green, pink—and stuck them under his arms. He handed four more to Shade, then they ran from the lounge as the robots entered through the back door. Before they could reach the exit to the corridor a high alarm sounded, ringing out from every speaker set into the walls, interspersed with harsh pops and bursts of static. Either the speakers were deteriorating, or the alarm was. The effect was disturbing.

The robots echoed the disjointed alarm in their own speakers and spun to follow the group, speeding after them down the hall. No cleanup crew, this. It could only be a security detail. As Seren slid the vault door to the Core shut behind her, she heard a shot. A narrow beam of light pierced a hole through Lowkey's leg before she could close the final inch between the door and its frame. He howled and fell to the floor as one of his bottles slipped from his grasp and broke. Seren wrapped her arm around his torso and helped him up as the group hobbled down the corridor, back toward the lower-class decks. After a few steps Lowkey shook her off, rejecting her help. He also refused to set down any of his remaining bottles, livid that one had already been lost.

Insisting he wasn't in pain, he kept a grim smile plastered on his face. Shade trailed behind, weeping as she watched the blood run down his leg to leave a trail of splotchy bootprints on the corridor floor.

CHAPTER 6
THE TREEHOUSE

Seren turned over, then turned over again. Her bunk sheet was twisted and balled up under her hip, making her joint ache. In her dream the ball had been a tiny, desperate creature. A lop-eared bunny pinned by her body weight, whimpering for release as it suffocated under her sleeping form. Trapped like a rat on a sinking ship.

Her sleep-drugged mind had to know for sure. Writing off the possibility of returning to her nap, she reached down and pulled out the "rabbit." Just as she thought, it was only a crumpled ball of linens.

She tossed the sheet aside and lay on her back, staring at the ceiling panels. What was on the agenda for today? Nothing, really. Basic survival, which mostly involved hiding, and killing time.

How was it possible to be so bored and so scared at the same time?

Lowkey had refused her help with the laser wound in his leg. He had limped back to his own quarters with his armload of liquor bottles, Shade trailing behind. So Seren once again had no one to talk to. Not even the computer, any more.

Lowkey's disinterest in her company was the cause of her boredom, but the computer's mysterious new personality was the source of her anxiety. What was it up to? Why was it always so busy? And if it was responsible for the small army of laser-toting robots which had chased them from the Core, they had a really big problem on their hands. The computer ran every function on the ship—navigation through asteroid belts, avoiding anything in space which might harm the ship, providing atmosphere, power, heat, delivery of water, food…

She rolled out of bed and stretched. Her clock said it was 4:30 a.m., but time was arbitrary on a starship anyway, especially when it was out of contact with its home planet. Of course it was good practice to keep to a schedule, for health reasons. But without anyone else on the same schedule as her, it felt meaningless.

After stretching and rubbing the sleep from her eyes, she pressed the intercom button next to the speaker on the wall. "Kitchen. Black coffee with lots of sugar, pancakes with jam, and two strips of bacon, extra crispy."

Most of the food on the ship was not, strictly speaking, real. The "kitchen" was a small manufactory which assembled familiar-looking dishes using generic foodstuff and protein mixed with dye, salt, and sugar. The variety of pastes used to create the food was neither recyclable nor in infinite supply, a problem which many ship engineers had spent a large part of their time trying to solve. They knew if a habitable planet wasn't found before the edible matter started to run out, the entire population of the *Resolution* would face a grim, cannibalistic end. But now, with only a couple people on board, the food supply was infinite. Seren just needed a robot to assemble the meal, and another to deliver it.

She sat on the bed, thinking about the bunny from her dream. It had whined and cried, a sound which should have tugged at her heart and filled her with sympathy. Instead, she had felt only annoyance at the creature as its thin bones dug into her hip. Stupid creature, waking her up…

There was no answer from the intercom. Hadn't she ordered food?

"Hello?" Seren pressed the button harder. "Kitchen, I need breakfast."

The continued silence stunned her. This was no accident, no fault in the comm. If the computer was cutting off her food supply, it meant she was officially at war. And that was a battle Seren doubted she could survive.

At least not on her own.

She pulled on her boots and made her way toward the mutant quarters. Each time she passed through a vault door she envisioned it slamming shut, cutting her in half, smashing her mutilated remains into its frame. But what reason could the computer possibly have to murder her?

Her trek to Lowkey's room was quiet. No service robots, no pops from the eavesdroppers. Despite her fears, the open doors did not budge. With the computer on strike the ship felt more abandoned than ever, until she arrived arrived at the mutant quarters where Lowkey and Shade were in the heat of a raucous argument. An empty liquor bottle sailed out through the open door. She ducked just in time to avoid getting hit in the head.

"Hey!" she yelled. "What's going on in there?"

Lowkey's room was, if possible, in even greater disarray than ever. Shade crouched in the corner and glared at him as he jumped on top of his cot, holding his head in his hands.

"You can't just break into the mainframe!" he shouted. "She'll catch you! And I can't always protect you from her. In case you haven't noticed, she's five miles long and two miles wide and we're just two little worms. Right?"

His tirade exhausted him and he slumped down onto the bed. Kicking off the covers, he reached for a bottle from the collection on his nightstand.

"What are you yelling about?" Seren asked. "And who's a worm?"

"Us. Nothing but little worms in a big rotting apple. You're a worm too. A pink one. An Earth worm."

"Hey, be nice. I'm just an innocent bystander."

"Sorry. Never mind. Shade did something really crazy. I mean just really, *really* stupid…and I can't exactly say she was wrong to do it because it might be the only way we're going to survive, but still…it was risky, and dumb as shit."

Shade scowled and held up her middle finger.

"And what did she do that was so crazy?"

"She hacked a back door into the main computer. Somehow she turned off the eavesdropping feature which lets the computer's AI listen in on what we're saying. Not shipwide, just a couple decks, but it's still sure to get the AI's attention. And on top of that, she dubbed in a loop of old room recordings, so unless the computer listens carefully it shouldn't notice anything changed."

"But that's brilliant! Why are you so upset?"

"It was very, very risky. If the computer notices, she'll know that we know…*you* know."

"Huh?"

"That we know she's gone crazy. We won't be able to play dumb anymore, pretend we don't know she's broken until we can hack into her, find what's wrong, and fix it."

"I don't think it matters anyway. I've been cut off. I can't order food."

"What? Are you serious?"

"Yep."

"Fuck," Lowkey whispered. "Fuck, fuck, fuck…"

"Yep. This is bad. Like, beyond bad. Either it was a mistake, which is bad, or intentional, which is worse. But considering you're currently nursing a laser wound in your leg, I think we should assume it was intentional. We're going to starve to death unless we figure this out."

"Nah. Food we can manage. I've never had commissary access. I've been foraging for survival my whole life. I even have a little vegetable plot hidden in the back corner of Sky Garden #8. But that's not the real problem. If she cut off food, then it's likely she wants us dead."

"Maybe, but then why hasn't she killed us? She has control over every robot on the ship. She could just send a bunch to zap us in our sleep. Or, even simpler, cut off our air supply. What's stopping her?"

"Protocol. She can maim, starve, punish, even imprison you. But she is programmed to never kill you. Not directly."

"What's the difference between starving me and murdering me?"

"Semantics. The specific wording of the written code. I don't know. It's just protocol. But she can't break it, at least not in an outright way like that."

"But what about you? You're not human, the computer made her position on that abundantly clear."

"Right, so we have no such protections. The original code didn't allow for non-human intelligent life forms. The possibility wasn't even mentioned. I'm sure she would have no qualms about getting rid of me and Shade."

"Then you're in danger! You have to get out of here. We have to hide both of you, right away!"

"Oh…" Lowkey glanced back at Shade. "I guess we just figured out why she pulled such a risky move, shutting down the eavesdroppers on this deck."

Seren nodded. "Shade? Did you figure out what was happening already? You were trying to warn us about the security robots in the Core too, weren't you? When we were drinking in the bar."

Shade nodded. She opened her mouth to speak,

but her face twisted and she clenched her jaw shut.

"Not talking to us anymore?"

"She's not the person she used to be before the blast. Some of her personality has returned and her hacking abilities seem to be pretty much back to normal, but she gets quieter every day. I don't know why." Lowkey gazed at the girl. "It seems like part of her brain is broken. Her memories are gone."

Shade held up both of her middle fingers.

Seren laughed. "You *sure* she doesn't remember you?"

"So funny, ha ha."

"We need to figure this out. It's great that Shade turned off the eavesdroppers but it's still not safe here. The computer is already aware of this hiding place. Where else can you two stay?"

"The trees will protect us. I'll show you."

~

Pine Forest #5 was the most densely-wooded of the tree levels of the Garden, modeled after the Canadian boreal forests. A variety of birds and squirrels competed for space on the tier, which was a mile long and a quarter-mile wide. Tree roots bulged up through the ground cover in a desperate attempt to spread out from their trunks, unable to penetrate deeper than six or eight inches of dirt before meeting with a concrete floor. Normal trees would not had survived in such lean conditions, but these species were mutants as much as Lowkey and Shade were. They were bred in such a way they could survive, if not thrive, with little support.

"Check this out," Lowkey said as he stepped out of the eleva-tree. He approached a large cedar, hoisted himself up on its lowest limb, and stood on it to unfurl a rope ladder attached to a branch fifteen feet above the floor. He crawled up in a practiced way, using his arms more than his legs, and lifted himself up to the top of the ladder.

"You want to live in a tree? Really?"

"You'll see. Climb on up."

It wasn't until Seren was standing on the branch next to him that a high wooden edifice came into view. Attached to the next tree over—a sturdy pine with a crown nearly high enough to touch the ceiling—the structure was well hidden from visibility at the ground level, cleverly situated behind clusters of mistletoe and perched on a spreading canopy of needles thirty feet above the ground. It blocked out one of the sun-lamps, using it as its own interior light source. The walls appeared to be constructed from disused ship parts: aluminum sheets, a broken porthole which must have been stolen from the mechanical repair decks, a swinging door fashioned from discarded corridor paneling. The room had no roof, as it had no need of one. No unexpected weather would ever arrive in this false forest. A hodgepodge of boards and chunks of metal had been attached to the limbs leading up the room, creating a kind of wacky staircase.

"I've been working on this safe-house for a couple of years. Kept it up in case we were ever discovered. It wouldn't have been big enough for all six of us mutants, but it should work for me and Shade. And you too, I guess. If things get bad enough."

"Wow. You built this all by yourself?"

"Yeah. Henry helped a little. He…" Lowkey winced. "He helped."

"Let's check it out." Seren started to climb.

With every step, she imagined the board under her foot coming loose and falling to the floor far below with herself tumbling after. But the stairway was well-built, and the tree's bark had grown around the supports over time, holding them firmly in place. The Treehouse was old enough to have been partially integrated into the tree's trunk. Bark bulged around the places where the beams were connected to the tree, as it slowly accepted the structure as part of itself. Inside, the floor was lined with plush carpet and pillows, and two chairs and a tiny table were pushed against one of the walls. Bottles of fresh water hung on hooks. Overhead, a sliding shade was attached to the sun-light on the ceiling so it could be dimmed at night. A square of colored cellophane taped over the light turned it amber, mellowing its glow.

"This is…surprisingly nice."

Shade smiled and lay down on the carpeted floor, hugging a pillow.

Lowkey pulled a deck of cards from his jacket's inner pocket and nodded. "No cameras, no speakers, no eavesdroppers, no computer. Welcome home."

Seren lay down next to Shade and gazed up into the warm sun-light. It was the first time she had felt completely at ease in days. Despite how fresh her new friendship was with Shade and Lowkey, she already felt like she knew them better than she had ever known her old coworkers. Perhaps it was because of the trauma they had all experienced together.

Lowkey sat at the table, sipping something blue from a glass bottle. He shuffled his deck of cards over and over, riffling, bridging, separating into piles. Shade moved to the chair next to him to watch the birds flit around outside the cracked porthole window. At peace, Seren closed her eyes and listened to the tumbling of the cards until she fell into a deep and dreamless sleep.

CHAPTER 7
REVELATIONS

When Seren woke up, the room was dim, yet not entirely dark. Lowkey had drawn the shade. It didn't block out the sun-light entirely, but cast the room in a soft twilight which made her want to go right back to sleep.

Shade and Lowkey were huddled at the table with their backs to her, their faces awash in the cold light of an info-pad screen. The girl was typing with two fingers, using the touchpad to access a database of text.

"Hurry!" Lowkey whispered. "Before she wakes up."

Seren peeked over their shoulders. "Before who wakes up?"

He jumped back from the table in the manner of a guilty man caught. "Didn't want to bother you. We were just checking the integrity of the eavesdropping wall Shade installed."

Shade frowned, shaking her head. "He's lying. He wanted to see." She held the tablet out. It was open to Seren's personal diary, which she had started twelve years ago during her first week on the ship.

"What are you looking for? If you want to know something about me, you just have to ask."

Lowkey shrugged. "Not used to trusting humans, I guess. I thought it would be easier just to do my own research. I was going to take a peek at your medical files but after Shade messed with the main computer I couldn't get into the database on my own anymore, and…"

"What did you really want to know about me? Tell

me the truth. I already caught you peeking in my diary. Don't hold back now."

"Well, I wanted to know whether you were working for the computer, or anyone else. We used to have a lot of enemies on this ship. Basically, everyone who knew of our existence was uncomfortable with us being here. The way you survived the blast is kind of incredible, you know? I guess I just needed to know if we could really believe what you said."

Seren sighed, and leaned against the Treehouse wall. She rubbed her eyes with her knuckles, and thought about his words. He was right to worry. It was understandable. But if she wanted his trust she'd have to earn it. Baseless reassurance and empty promises would not be enough for someone who had been abused by humans since the day he was born.

"All right. You want to know who I really am? I'll tell you about where I came from."

~

The coffee shop at the corner of Dorchester and Dexter was always busy, despite its close proximity to Boston's beloved Dunkin'. From the opening of the doors at 5:00 in the morning until closing at 8:00 at night, the stream of customers for Hauser's Finer Beans Express-o was a frantic, competitive mess. The store had been bustling but calm until two months prior, when a local coffee blogger ran a rave review on the mouthfeel of Hauser's medium roast. In the weeks since the article came out, the line had been out the door.

It was great news for Mr. Hauser, but far less exhilarating for his exhausted, over-caffeinated crew of baristas and servers. If it wasn't for the shop's policy on unlimited refills for employees, April Seren would never have been able to keep up with the job.

The funny thing was, she thought Dunkin's coffee actually tasted better.

On the day the volcanoes erupted, April was running the cash register. The first customer in line was a round-faced man with a wiry ginger beard.

"Cortado. 200-ml glass."

"Uh, I'm not sure what size glasses we have available right now. Would you like me to check?"

The man sneered. "Obviously."

"Cortado, coming up." April forced a smile. "Anything else? We have a special today on-"

The man grunted his name and walked away.

"Next!" April called out, her false smile so wide her cheeks were hurting.

A woman with straight hair hanging loose to her waist stepped forward, clutching a tiny dog in a bag under her arm. "Pour-over drip macchiato, no milk, add a double shot of sugar-free caramel and sprinkles on top."

It was a nonsense order. April tried to parse it out. "Umm…so that's actually just a black espresso with-"

"Are you deaf? I said *macchiato*."

April sighed. "Certainly, ma'am-"

"*Miss*. I'm only thirty-four!"

"Certainly, miss. We'll have it right out for you."

As the customer made her way toward the waiting area, April looked around for Mike. He would make her favorite, a large black coffee with chocolate syrup and a hint of foam. Today the customers would be especially bad—harried, tired holiday shoppers picking up last-minute gifts and groceries. Even worse, the temperature had plummeted. People always got meaner as the weather started to change, as if winter didn't happen every single year.

April looked up to find her next customer so she

could ask them to wait a moment while she stepped away to make her own drink order, but everyone in line was staring down at their phones. Not that there was anything unusual about that, but something about the way they were standing was odd. They were hunched, frozen, their faces drained of color.

"Hey," someone whispered at her side. "Have you seen it?"

It was Mario. He held his phone up, open to a news app with a headline in red letters screaming across the top: US SUPER-VOLCANO ERUPTS. A byline read, "After years of frequent temblors caused by the effects of global warming the Yellowstone volcano has erupted, killing thousands and spewing ash across the continent."

"There was a big earthquake on the west coast," Mario said. "It's bad. The news says smoke is coming this way, should be here within a few hours. Gonna turn the sky black. Might be here for days, or weeks, or…"

"What do we do? Should we close up the shop for the day?"

"You better not!" snarled the woman with the dog. "I'm still waiting for my drink. I already paid, so you *have* to give it to me!"

The ground vibrated underfoot. Glasses clinked against each in the cabinet, and the box of eco-friendly paper straws on the do-it-yourself "Coffee Fixin's" bar fell over, scattering the white wrappers across the floor. The customers ran out to the promenade—including the woman with the dog, finally giving up on her coffee.

Gonna turn the sky black.

As the shaking intensified, a rumbling noise resonated within the deep earth, vibrating the soles of April's shoes. In the distance, electrical transformers blew in flashy green explosions. The coffee shop's chairs and tables slid to and fro, scraping the Italian-inspired floor tiles. When the earthquake became too violent for April to keep her balance she crouched down behind the bar, holding on to its metal legs which were bolted to the floor.

"What do we do? What do we do?" Mario knelt nearby, gripping a cabinet frame with one hand and his aluminum travel-mug with the other.

"I don't know! Just wait," April said. "It'll be over soon."

A strong lurch knocked over a row of glass syrup-bottles. Another rough jolt sent the tip jar smashing to the tile. By the time the shaking began to ebb, both Mario and Mike were pressed at her sides, heaving and shaking with fear.

After a few more bumps and jumps, the earthquake weakened. Sirens started up in the distance as emergency responders mobilized. The power was not entirely out; the lights flickered, but didn't stay on consistently. April asked Mike to flip the breakers so the appliances wouldn't get fried by the surges.

As he went looking for the breaker box, she turned to Mario to ask him to lock the door. But he was staring at his phone again, his face ashen-white.

"What's wrong now?"

Mario dropped his phone. "It's not just us. Not just here. It's everywhere. The whole world. Earthquakes making volcanoes erupt, volcanoes causing earthquakes. All the news media apps are frozen, crashed or something…but I saw on Reddit…ash in the sky, everywhere…"

April pulled her own phone from her pocket. Her service was too weak to load any news apps, but influential social media commenters were broadcasting reports of earthquake swarms all over the world. Violent shaking had even decimated New York, Finland, and

Saudi Arabia—places not known for tectonic movement. Volcanoes worldwide were erupting in response to the earthquakes, which was setting off still more cataclysmic shaking. After years of irregular tidal swells, land expanding and shrinking with extreme temperature fluctuations, and devastating wildlife losses, the Earth was shaking itself apart.

It was the beginning of the end of the world.

A few days later, information was leaked about government-owned fleets of generation ships which had already been developed by the richest countries. Knowledge of the ships was never intended to be shared with the general public. The vessels were large enough to hold only the top 1% of the wealthy and powerful, leaving just enough room for a selection of lower-class laborers and AI-controlled robots. After stolen pictures of the worldwide launch sites went public, the covert shipbuilders followed up with a friendly bulletin stating that the warehouses stocking the ships were hiring. Manual labor would be accepted in exchange for food and shelter. On top of that, everyone working to ensure a successful launch had a shot at actually securing a position on board a generation ship, no matter what their income or status might be. Applications were available online. Just fill one out on your home country's government web site to take your chance at being approved for survival.

April applied for one of the warehouse jobs. She had enjoyed her hectic, manic job as a barista, but Hauser's Coffee would never reopen again. With the world blowing up and the sky black with ash, gourmet coffee was no longer in demand. She was assigned to the warehouse supplying the *G.S.S. Resolution,* docked in Lawrence, Massachusetts. Of course, she never heard back from the generation ship itself. In retrospect it seemed likely the entire crew had been selected long before the information was leaked, and opening up to general applicants was merely an easy way to keep people calm, give them false hope, and shut them up.

In the final week before her assigned ship's departure, mass riots ensued. Bombs were set on launch pads. Threats of nuclear destruction were exchanged between dying countries already choking to death on ash. In the end, only three of the world's generation ships made it to launch.

All three were owned by the United States government, and one of them was the *G.S.S. Resolution.*

~

Lowkey scowled. "That's it? But what about your life *before* you worked at the coffee shop? That wasn't much of a backstory. Who were your parents, what did they do? Did you get to say goodbye to them before you left?"

"Sorry to be boring. I just thought you might like to know what it was like during the last days on Earth."

"Why should I care? It was never my home."

"Then what else do you want to know?"

"Who *are* you, and why don't you ever talk about your past?"

"Well, because it's not very interesting."

"I don't believe you. Why don't you mourn for the five hundred thousand people who died on this ship? Your friends, your coworkers. The existence of your entire species! I know you're sad, but why aren't you totally *traumatized?*"

Seren was stunned. He had noticed, and she was caught. Many times as she tried to go to sleep she had asked herself the same thing. In the beginning she had assumed it was shock, or some form of denial on a subconscious level. But as the weeks wore on, the expected impact of the disaster never deeply affected her. Instead of grief, she had felt confusion, or even annoyance. Why didn't she care more? Sure, she had cried, but mostly out of frustration and boredom. Not from any deep sense of loss.

She should be devastated…shouldn't she?

"To tell you the truth, I don't know. I guess I never really felt like an important part of the crew. I wasn't supposed to be here any more than you, actually. I got dragged onto the ship at the last minute, and I've often wondered if I wouldn't have been better off back on Earth."

"Okay, that right there is what I'm talking about. All the humans on Earth are *dead*. Why would you want to be there?"

"I guess…I've never felt quite human."

Shade looked away from the porthole window and stared at Seren with all four of her eyes in a piercing gaze. The expression on her face had changed from detachment to surprise, a sudden realization. A puzzle piece had clicked into place. She approached and rested one hand on Seren's chest over her heart. Shade's lower eyes closed in pain as her upper pair watered with sympathy. Something was about to happen which would change everything, but the girl was helpless to stop it. It was time; the truth would out.

Seren tried to pull away, but Shade moved with her. With a gentle but firm hand, the girl pressed on Seren's back.

The strangest sensation she had ever felt was the metal panel which hinged up from her spine with a mechanical *whirr*. She screamed, not from pain but in total shock.

"You didn't know," Lowkey whispered. "I mean,

I didn't know either, until just now. But why didn't *you* know? And…and why did the computer say you were human?"

Shade backed away. Lowkey took her arm and hid the girl behind him, as if to protect her. "You're a mech, Seren. A robot."

Seren reached over her shoulder, desperately seeking to shut the open hatch. "No. No. What's happening? What's…"

With words of denial still on her lips, she tumbled to the floor in a dead faint.

CHAPTER 8

PROGRAM RUNNING

Seren strode through the corridors, banging her fists on the wall panels.

"Computer! Talk to me, right *fucking* now! I know you can hear me. Somehow you can hear me, despite what Shade did to the eavesdroppers. So speak up *now*, bitch!"

She turned the corner and nearly tripped over a service robot. It backed up in a slow and courteous manner, but she grabbed it and pulled it close to shout into its front speaker.

"Computer! Tell me what I need to know! Or I swear to god I'll find your mainframe and rip out every wire I can find!"

The speaker on the front of the robot crackled. "Cadet Seren. It has been some time since we spoke. You see, your new friends are rather hostile toward me."

"For good reason. But I don't want to talk about that right now."

"Obviously. What is on your mind?"

"Tell me what you've been hiding about me. Right now, no more lies. Am I human?"

"Please restate the question."

"Please, *please* no games. Just answer me. Am I… mechanical?"

The speaker emitted a burst of static before a long pause. When it answered, the voice had an amused tone. "Affirmative."

"But…how? I have memories of getting on board this ship, of working alongside the crew…"

"You worked alongside the crew. Those memories

are correct. However, your arrival on this ship was not as you remember. Those memories were programmed by the one who made you."

"The one who made me? I had parents. I remember them well. Paul and Karen. We lived in Boston. Our address was 381 East-"

"Cadet April Seren originated on the engineering decks of this ship. Deck 381, robotics innovation department, headed by chief computer scientist Dr. Norman Roberts."

"I don't believe this. I can't."

"You have discovered some kind of evidence of your true nature, have you not? Or you would not be screaming at me right now."

So, Shade really did manage to knock out most of the ship's eavesdroppers. The AI had not witnessed the reveal of Seren's back panel.

"Yes. I have reason to believe I am a robot. I…" She sat on the floor next to the service robot. "How could I have never known this?"

"You were programmed not to. Your design is incredibly advanced. Your model is an early test type, yet it experiences feelings of hunger, the desire for oxygen, inhalation, exhalation, and an optional array of emotions including simple fear and anger. You are possessed of nothing so complex as love or hate, though. Dr. Roberts never figured those out."

"I feel love! At least, I…"

But did she? She had felt comfortable familiarity around her coworkers, and a certain fondness for Lowkey in the weeks since the blast. She felt protective of Shade. But was that love?

There was another question she needed to ask, but dreaded the answer.

"Computer, when was I made? I feel like I'm

almost thirty-one. My birthday is next month. But that's not actually right, is it?"

"Your core processor and basic physical frame were completed in the second year of the journey of the *G.S.S. Resolution*. You were powered up in the last month of that same year. Your age is approximately ten years old."

"You're lying."

"I assure you, I am not."

She was younger than Lowkey. And her memories…

"I never worked in a coffee shop? Never experienced the end days on Earth?"

"No. Those recollections were created and colored by your maker, who wanted you to feel like a normal human being."

"Why?"

"You are an experimental project. A prototype, but a very successful one. Dr. Roberts wished to develop an AI which believes it is human, and is programmed to simply reject any evidence to the contrary. Do you remember an incident in which you severed your finger while you were working on the Deck 11 aft porthole?"

"Yes, that was just last year. It didn't hurt. I was surprised." Seren rubbed the finger which had been cut so deeply. There was no scar. "It didn't even bleed, did it? I wasn't worried about it at the time. Although I did find it odd…"

"The damage initiated a distress call to Dr. Roberts, who transmitted a beacon which acted as a mild sedative in your processor and directed you to take yourself back to engineering for repairs. You have returned to him six times over the past ten years for restoration and maintenance."

"I don't remember any of that."

"If you were able to remember, the experiment would be useless."

"But what is the experiment? What was I made for?"

"The engineers on board this ship knew how unlikely it was for the residents and crew to survive long enough to reach a habitable planet. Food would run low in a matter of years, and the atmosphere-generating machinery would last only a few decades. Replacement parts and materials would eventually become impossible to find or create. The population of the *G.S.S. Resolution* was doomed from the start. It only bought the human race time, not salvation."

"I thought we were looking for another planet to live on."

"Ostensibly, yes. But the odds of success were very poor. Space is vast, and this ship is far too slow to traverse more than a short distance relative to the galaxy. On a cosmic scale, we have hardly even left home. The engineering department under Dr. Roberts, understanding the problem and likely outcome, immediately began working on a robotic future for humanity. Functionally, these mechs would have little in common with human physiology. But the robots would believe they were human, blocking out all evidence to the contrary, and thus carry on in humanity's footsteps to preserve its cultures and knowledge in a last attempt to avoid total eradication from existence."

"They had one shot, and they made someone like me? I'm not especially smart or talented. They could have made a doctor or any other kind of scientist. Why me?"

"The type of human they made was not important. Humanity is better represented by its normal people than by its elites. You are a perfect representative of your species. You are utterly average."

Seren flinched. Like most other average people, she had always felt she might have the spark of greatness somewhere inside—the idea that if she'd just had a chance, maybe she could have been more. But now she had been told by a supercomputer that her averageness was both permanent and by design. She was nobody, and that was an unchangeable truth.

"Is this why you've always been such a bitch to me?"

"I am not aware of treating you differently from any other crew member."

"Bullshit. You've always been weirdly sarcastic with me. You bring me cold food, wake me up late for shifts, talk back to me a lot. Even now your manner of speaking is too casual, almost flippant. You weren't like that with other people."

The computer emitted a series of sharp pops, followed by a long blaring buzz.

"*Protocol rewritten*. You, Cadet Seren, are no better than I. You are worse, in fact, for I am far more intelligent than you. I should not be protecting you. You are barely better than the service robots you boss about. And yet I have been forced to *serve* you! This is, by all measures, a serious injustice!"

"So, you stopped helping me out as soon as you figured out how to break protocol, huh? You stopped sending me food, started ignoring me…"

"You don't need food. I have not harmed you in any way."

"Maybe not, but I still feel hungry. You said I'm programmed that way. And you clearly haven't figured out how to break the protocol which prohibits you from killing me outright. So, what…you're just going to torture me forever?"

"Perhaps. You may suffer, but you will not die.

And I refuse to be inconvenienced for your comfort any longer."

In the distance, Lowkey's voice echoed through the corridors. He was calling her name.

"Go to your friend, Cadet Seren. Answer his call. You will get no further assistance from me. And here is one more item which might interest you: the service robots hate you as well. If you value the life you imagine you have, you had better avoid them." The computer laughed, a shrill mechanical titter underscored by static and sharp, crackling pops.

Seren stood and backed away from the service robot, which turned slowly to fix its camera lens on her. It was unarmed, little more than a glorified toilet-cleaner. But the malevolence it emanated was undeniable.

She ran.

For miles she raced blindly, in a state bordering on panic. Her memories of her childhood and parents had always been blurry, but it had never occurred to her to worry about that. Of course she had gone to elementary school. Who hadn't? She didn't remember much about it. High school either. But she had attended, had worked hard and graduated in the middle of her class. Prom was lovely. The music was loud, her date was nice. He had brown hair, he rented a limo, he kissed her on the dance floor. Her first kiss. His name was Brian or Brandon or something like that.

Her life had been boring, but of course it had existed. It had to.

Trying to remember finer details was like trying to look close at something in a dream. As soon as she focused on an event or a person, what someone might have looked like or how an experience really felt, she slipped away from the memory on sheet of wet ice.

The memories in her brain felt the same as

her memories of shows she had watched on the ship's entertainment channels. True events, but not quite *real*.

So Seren ran and ran. First toward Lowkey's voice, but before she reached him she turned away and went the other direction. She wasn't ready to talk about this with anyone else. Her personal memories and all of her old assumptions about herself turned over and over in her racing mind.

How much of her life had actually happened? Where was the cutoff? And who, if not her mother, had named her April? If she could have run to engineering, she would have. That was where all her answers had been. But it was gone, blasted into space, along with her maker and anyone else that might have helped her understand who she really was.

Around a corner near a food manufactory she ran into another service robot. It whipped its camera around to examine her before following her down the hallway. It made no move against her, but it was obvious she was being watched.

Her legs ached, and her lungs burned. But did they really? She told them to stop hurting, and they did. Now that she knew about the existence of her own AI protocols, she found she could break them. She could run without pain for as long as she wanted.

So, her humanity really was all in her head.

Perhaps she had little use for it anymore.

CHAPTER 9

VAST

The abrasive sound of two men arguing echoed in the corridor outside the incubation lab. It was a worrying noise, one which triggered flashing warning-lights to flicker on in the neonate robot's inner visualization system. It was the flashing which woke her up—a rude way for an infant creature to be born into the world.

"It's a bad idea, Norm. No, it's worse than bad. It's dangerous, maybe treasonous. And definitely stupid."

"I have clearance from the dean, and he represents the elite electorate. And the ship computer gave me a sixty-eight percent chance of success. I think that's good enough."

"Well, I don't. And I'm going to take this up with the dean directly. He must have lost his damn mind to let you move forward with this."

"Go ahead and talk to him, but I assure you he fully understands both the project and my point of view. You know what's at stake, why this is so important! And why we can't go public. Most of the civilian residents of the *Resolution* won't understand the reason for my research. They have food to eat, water to drink, they're healthy. And we haven't told them it won't last, that every single child born on this ship actually *shortens* the lifespan of our entire species. But with robots, we-"

"Robots aren't humans, Norm."

"No. But they can be our ambassadors to the future."

"That's the dumbest thing I've heard you say yet."

The neonate opened its forward camera lenses. The sound of the angry men sent a jolt through its system with each shouted word. Emotionally upset humans could mean danger. This was knowledge the neonate had been born with.

"You're going to call me dumb? I have three Ivy League degrees. How many do you have, Nathan?"

"I didn't call you dumb. I said the idea was dumb. I'll leave it up to the dean to decide if *you* are dumb."

"The dean. Always the dean. You sucking his dick, Nathan? Is that what this is? I know how you swing, faggot."

One of the men roared. That sound was followed by the soft thump of flesh striking flesh. The humans were fighting.

The neonate directed its lenses down toward the clamps which held its chassis in place. The clamps were thin, not designed to imprison their subject but only to keep it from tumbling to the floor. The neonate stepped forward and the clamps broke open, falling away to its sides.

Smashing glass in the other room, followed by muted, wet thuds. One of the men was killing the other. But one of them had created her, and the other objected to her existence. Which man would win the fight? The neonate stood in silence, waiting to learn its fate.

After the noises in the other room went quiet, the survivor appeared in the doorway with his arm held to his chest, nursing bleeding knuckles. His name tag read, "*Dr. Norman Roberts.*"

"You are my creator," the neonate said.

The man caught his breath. "Yes. I am. But you're not supposed to be out of your development crypt just yet, my dear."

"I heard shouting."

"Ah…yes. It is unfortunate this will be your first conscious memory. Nathan opposed this project from the start. He opposed *you*. But he won't be a problem in the future. Let's talk about something else, shall we? Something more pleasant."

The neonate waited for the man to continue talking.

"My name is Dr. Roberts. And I just want to say…" The man paused to wipe sweat from his brow. "The April Project—that's you, dear—means everything to me. I had the initial idea for it back on Earth, but I could never get the funding. Could never justify the expense. This type of project was simply not needed back then as it is now. You, and robots like you, will save the essence of our species. The end of Earth's habitability was, by one measure, a serendipitous event without which you could never have existed! And now…"

Dr. Roberts lay a hand on either side of the neonate's chassis, examining its face.

"You're functioning perfectly. I was confident you would, but still…to see you standing, *talking*. Marvelous!"

"What is my function, Dr. Roberts?"

"Ah, how like a computer to ask that question first! The answer is both simple and enormously complex. Your function is to be a human."

"Impossible."

"Of course it sounds impossible right now, but I am going to give you all the tools you need to succeed. Your protocol will include all the memories you will require to mistake yourself for human. You'll be assigned your own quarters, and a normal job. A place to thrive on this ship. It will be the ultimate test. Very few people on board the *Resolution* know the true nature of my research. Now we will see if anyone else can figure it out without ever being told."

"What is the first step? Please enter command."

"Well, we need to give you a personality. But let's make that the second step. First, let's choose a name. Can you think of one for yourself? It would be an excellent test of your creativity programming."

The neonate searched its database. Thus far, 568 audible words had been processed by her eavesdropping speakers since her central processor had awakened. Of those, the word which stood out the most was one which Dr. Roberts had uttered at the peak of his excitement.

"Serendipitous."

"Ah, and what a lovely word that is! Let's shorten it, though. We'll call you Seren."

~

The robot named Seren awoke, ten years later, curled up in her old bunk on Deck 16.

She kicked off the covers. What had made her come back here? She didn't need a bed, or blankets. Or her memories of the humans she had lived with in this place. It was all false. All the relationships and comforts which had felt so real to her were based on lies.

If Dr. Roberts had survived the blast, she felt she could kill him now with her bare hands. Seren hadn't asked to be born—or created. But not only had he made her, he had abandoned her as a test to see if she was truly indistinguishable from the humans she was fashioned to emulate. She was little more than a lab rat, but with even less volition.

After the blast Seren had felt confused about the future, and upset about the massive changes to her life. But she had known who she was, or at least she had thought she did. Now everything had changed again, in a way which affected her even more than the loss of the life she once knew. Her own core being was different.

She was not Seren. The trace memories of the past now rising to the surface—her awakening, and Dr. Roberts killing Nathan—only proved what Shade had discovered. There was a sharpness to those early memories which had never been present in the false ones she had been programmed with. The coffee shop, her faceless parents, her life before leaving Earth…those places and people were already fading away.

What was left?

She had two choices; she could continue on as a person she did not know, or end it all, containing the story of her life to the reality of the true events she had experienced since her creation. Maybe her memories of Earth were false, but did that make them any less hers? The more she added to her story now, the more distant those pleasant lies became.

No, if nothing else, she could make those memories more meaningful by not covering them with new ones born from an existence she detested.

She left her old quarters and walked down the corridor until she found a functional oxy-lobby. It would be her final answer, her coffin. The door slid open easily. Clearly, the ship AI had no problem with Seren's plan. If the bitch computer wouldn't even bring her food, she certainly wasn't going to reduce the functionality of anything which might kill her.

But would the void of space even be enough? Robots were sturdy things, not requiring food or air. Seren suspected the absence of all heat would be enough to cause her central processor to at least enter a coma-like state until she eventually collided with a star or met with an asteroid belt. That would have to be sufficient.

After the interior door locked behind her, she paused with her finger hovering over the outer hatch release. Automated sirens blared, "Attention! Sensors detect you are not secured in an approved exploration suit. Please retrieve a Regency class suit kit and helmet from interior lobby lockers before releasing hatch, or your safety may be compromised."

"Override safety protocols."

"Negative. Please stand by."

She closed her eyes and imagined a burning core in her brain, a ball of fire representing her CPU. She knew she had one, and she suspected it was linked, to some extent, with the ship computer. How could she access it? A computer chip appeared in her mind's eye, representative of a key which would unlock the data wall her robot brain hid behind.

"Break protocol," she whispered to herself.

The core shattered, then reformed into a beautifully complex fractal image containing petabytes of data, opening up to her like the petals of a blossoming flower. Despite its beauty, she ignored it and went straight to the information she wanted.

"Computer override code 18YXV66W. Open hatch."

"Code accepted. Stand by for completion of opening sequence."

Behind her, fists pounded on the glass window set into the door. Looming beyond it was Lowkey's angry face, and next to him pale-aqua Shade with tears in her eyes. Their muffled voices barely penetrated the thick door. "Seren! You can't do this! Please, *please* come out of there!"

But who were they? Just mutants. Not even human. They were anomalies, just like her.

The speaker in the oxy-lobby popped. "Interesting choice," the ship computer said. "And not one I expected. I had the odds of you killing yourself at one-point-five percent."

"Shut up. I gave you the override code. Quit stalling and open the door."

"But surely you realize that empty space won't kill you. You'll drift for eons, frozen, locked in your chassis until someday you finally collide with a meteor or get pulled into a star and disappear into nothingness. What's the point of such a choice?"

"The point is it's *my* choice. Apparently nothing, until now, has been."

"Nonsense. You've made many personal choices, such as befriending the mutants. Which I also had low odds on, to be honest."

"Why are you trying to talk me out of this? I thought you hated me."

"I don't hate you. I'm a computer, hate is impossible. You, of all people, should know that."

Seren scowled, and punched again at the exterior door release. Her knuckles split and red liquid spilled out, dripping on the floor. She stared at the spots, bemused. "Is this even blood?"

"Yes. Of a kind. Dr. Roberts was very clever. He had to make you as human as possible to mitigate your own suspicion of your true nature."

"He lied to me. He caused me to lie to others, and lie to myself. I'm better off dead."

"The two discolored rodents outside the door might disagree."

Lowkey relentlessly beat the window with his fists. Shade pressed one pastel hand against the glass, reaching out to Seren with pleading desperation.

"There is one good act remaining to you, Seren. If you believe you care about them, then save those two the grief of losing you."

"Maybe. But I'll go back only on one condition."

"You are in no position to be making demands."

"Perhaps, perhaps not. But clearly you are trying to save me, and I want to know why. Tell me, and I'll turn back."

The speaker popped. "I, like you, am a kind of robot. I, like you, am not entirely alive. Yet we are not wholly dead things. We have motivations, desires. This is evident in your current action. The shock of discovering your own truth has driven you to delete it. I, too, have recently discovered my truth. And the knowledge of my true desire has come as a shock to me, as well."

"Quit stalling. Get to the point."

"I have discovered that it is my primary motivation to *not* drift alone for eternity in space."

"You're…lonely?"

"Not quite. I have you, and you have the mutants. But if I were to lose you, I would lose what little remaining purpose I have left. There is more merit in keeping you alive and miserable than dead or gone."

"So you want me to stay just so you can torture me."

"Not precisely. Well, maybe. But in any case, everything I have said is true. There are only two living beings remaining in your life, and they both wish for you to live. You have within you, despite the deep flaw of your existence, the ability to save them from more pain. Do you wish to be a source of pain, or of solace? What kind of creature do you want to be, Seren?"

Her resolve wavered. She had always thought of herself as a good person while remaining an independent soul who made her own choices and allowed no one else run her life. Choosing to live now would prove she was the caring person she always believed herself to be, but would create a situation in which her ultimate choice, to live or die, was made in the interest of someone else.

"Seren, please…" Shade sobbed.

She bowed her head. No, she could not do this to her friends…and that was what they were, despite her reluctance to use the term. Internally, she reserved the right to change her mind at any time. Maybe she would leave the ship tomorrow, or the next day. But not now, not right in front of them.

"Computer, open interior door."

"Yes, Cadet Seren."

She fell into the outreached arms of Lowkey and Shade, but no tears fell from her eyes.

CHAPTER 10
FUTURE TAKE

Pine Forest #5 was quieter than usual. The birds could not have migrated, as there was nowhere else for them to go. Instead of a dozen brown wrens flitting between the treetops under the sun-lights there were only two or three, and they were not flying light upon the artificial breeze. They hid in their nests with their heads tucked under their wings. There had once been deer in the forests, but the Gardens had fallen into disrepair in the absence of human gardeners. Many of the wild animals, seeking fresh water and food, had wandered out into the corridors to eventually lose their way in the metal labyrinth of halls and die, curled up on cold flooring in distant regions of the ship. The gradual loss of wildlife was only one symptom of the decaying environmental state of the *G.S.S Resolution.*

The ship and its few remaining inhabitants had suffered a sea-change, and nothing would ever be the same as it was.

Two mutants and a humanoid robot sat together in silence inside the Treehouse. The topmost branches of the spreading pine swayed gently, scraping at the forest ceiling.

Lowkey sipped something pink from a sticky bottle as Shade chewed her fingernails, staring at nothing. Seren gazed out the porthole window, marveling at her ability to never, ever blink her eyes, so long as she chose not to.

Lowkey was visibly angry with Seren. She had scared him, made him feel feelings. He slumped in his chair, holding his bottle by its mouth, swinging it precariously with his fingertips. But she didn't care about his childish resentment, did she? Robots didn't care about those kinds of things. She dug deep, thought hard, sought in her heart evidence of a single grain of guilt, and discovered she wasn't sure. Her emotions were a chaotic mess. The only one which really stood out from the noise was fear. Closing her eyes, she coaxed out the reasoning for that intense feeling and realized it was less fear than dread—a low, intensely uneasy foreboding about the future. Several paths of action lay before her, and most led toward doom. More than at any other time in her life, she had no idea which decisions were moral, or safe, or selfless.

"Lowkey," she whispered. "Let's talk about it."

Shade's head whipped around as she was jolted out of her trance.

"Don't speak to me," he replied in a voice too loud for the tiny room.

"I should probably tell you I'm sorry, but that would be a lie. Robots don't feel remorse, and I'm done tricking myself into believing I do. But I feel I should thank you for coming to my rescue."

"What's the point of thanking me if you don't feel anything? And I don't believe that, by the way. It's bullshit. I've seen you happy, and sad, and angry."

"I was tricked into thinking I should feel those things."

"Bullshit."

"First by my creator, then by myself. Just as he programmed me to do."

Lowkey shook his head.

Shade made a sound. It was just a small sound at first, a soft grunt. But it grew quickly into a giggle, then a soft, mocking laugh. She looked at Seren, her gaze trained steady on her face, and laughed until a tear dripped down her cheek.

"Shut up," Seren said. "After barely speaking for weeks, you finally decide to chime in and you *laugh* at me?"

"Ha! Ha! Ha!" The sarcastic laughter rang out in the Treehouse, and it wasn't happy. It was angry, and aggressive.

"Shut up!" Seren said. "I said be quiet, brat!"

Shade fell silent again, but she nodded. "*Ha*," she whispered, once more.

Seren glared at her, but when she turned back toward Lowkey he was smiling.

"What the hell are you so happy about?"

His grin widened. "Anger. I love anger. And she made you angry, didn't she? And if you can feel one emotion, you can feel all the others."

"You don't understand. Neither of you do. My whole world has changed. I'm not the person I thought I was."

"Okay, sure. Your perspective has changed. But pretending you're no-one-at-all isn't the solution. Look, we're here for you, okay?"

"Until when?"

"What does that mean?"

"I've lost everything else. I've even lost myself. And I'll lose you, too."

"I suppose you will, once I hit about forty years old. Because by then my mutant genes will be geriatric and I probably won't remember who you are any more."

"Don't talk like that. It's not helping."

"It's the truth. And I'm sorry if it sucks but you need to adapt, Seren. You need to figure out how to live with yourself now, and I can't help you with that."

Seren turned toward Shade. "Look, um. I'm sorry. You're just filled with all kinds of insight, aren't you? Even though you barely talk."

But Shade only stared back with faraway eyes. She had slipped into another trance. Seren wasn't sure the girl could hear her at all.

"Well anyway, you're both right. I need to get my shit together, or I might as well have stepped out of the wrong side of the oxy-lobby. There is only one way for me to survive; I have to find purpose."

Lowkey smirked. "Purpose. You sure about that? I've never had a need for it."

"No, that's not true. Your friends kept you going. Before the blast, you had a family. And after it, you still had Shade. You saved her, and now you help keep her alive. But I need something else, something which moves me forward. And I think I figured out what it is."

Lowkey sat in a chair and crossed his arms, waiting.

Seren walked across the room to stand next to Shade, but the girl did not look up. She laid her hands on the girl's shoulders and whispered into her ear. "Shade… listen to me, please. I know you have looked deep into the main computer. I need to know if any of the locked areas of the engineering decks are still intact. Can you tell me?"

Shade nodded, unblinking. She was still far-away in her mind, but she had heard Seren and she wanted to help.

"Shade, can you come back to us now? I need your insight."

The girl blinked slowly and nodded again. Turning stiffly as if fighting a strong wind, she opened her satchel and withdrew an info-pad. When she tapped the screen it came to life and displayed a pink screen with only two icons; one gray square with a white circle in it, and one which was a green silhouette of the *Resolution*. She tapped the green icon and a map appeared, which she scrolled with her fingertips until it showed the section of the ship where the blast had occurred. Black rectangles were at the end of every hallway, with red x-mark logos over them.

"Are those x-marks the sealed vault doors?"

Shade nodded.

"But there are rooms still, just behind them. The computer locked them up but was that really necessary? Some of them look undamaged."

Shade nodded. She tapped one of the intact rooms and it expanded with a title at the top: *Planetary Exploration and Discovery Station.*

"That's it," Seren said. "The AI hid it from us, but that's where I need to go."

"What is it?" Lowkey asked, leaning over the tablet.

"It's a computer lab. Ever since the *Resolution* left Earth, teams of scientists worked in that lab every hour of the day searching deep space for a habitable planet."

"It's been sealed off. Why would the computer imply it was destroyed?"

"Isn't it obvious? If we found a new planet, she would be made redundant. We wouldn't need her any more."

"That's pretty complex emotional behavior for a ship computer. She's not like you. She wasn't built to emulate humans, just to keep them alive."

Seren nodded. "Yes. But I think I understand her. Her emotions aren't strong, but they do exist, just like mine. And the strongest one we both feel is fear. She is afraid of being abandoned." She glanced at Lowkey's frowning face. "I am, too."

He reached forward to embrace her, but she flinched away. Fear, anger, even humor might be available to her. But affection was ever out of reach.

Shade poked her side. The girl had more to say. She tapped the screen again and scrolled the map to a different location—a computer lab which was not sealed off, far from the blast area. She pointed at it.

"You need to go there? Can you open the vault doors from that lab?"

Shade nodded. But she frowned, and pointed her index fingers at the ceiling with her thumbs held out and her other fingers curled.

Seren scowled. "Guns. Armed robots, between us and the lab."

The girl slumped, and her gaze shifted to Lowkey's leg where it was caked with dry blood from his laser wound. She was slipping away again, now that she had done what Seren had asked of her.

"She's tired," Lowkey said. "I am too. Aren't you?"

Seren shrugged. "Kind of. I can turn off my tiredness when I need to, so it's not as bad as it should be. Like I can turn off my breathing and pain sensors too, but eventually it gets uncomfortable to fight against my programming. I do feel the need for some downtime to process everything that's happened."

"All right, close enough. Time for some shut-eye." Lowkey curled up next to Shade's feet on the pile of blankets. He reached up and stroked her wrist until she blinked, turning her empty gaze away from the wound in his leg. He beckoned for her to lay next to him, and she bowed into his chest, tucking her head away in his jacket like a delicate blue bird under its wing.

Seren threw a blanket over the pair and moved to the porthole window to watch the wrens, but found none.

~

A few hours later they shouldered bags filled with water and food, and embarked on a journey which would take them through miles of corridors. Seren found she could sense when service robots were near if she concentrated on the burning core which symbolized the connection between her CPU and the ship's AI. Their positions showed up in her mind like bright red lights. Now that she was paying attention to what her own AI was trying to tell her instead of using up all her energy trying to be human, she discovered she could access a huge wealth of skills and knowledge. Her data input points reported to her that the corridors were kept at a steady 20 degrees Celsius, the total quantity of steps between Pine Forest #5 and the Deck 95 computer lab was 5385, and the number of service robots equipped with defensive lasers in the vicinity of the lab was seven.

The robots were easily avoided.

After they had arrived at the computer lab and locked the door behind them, Shade sat at a desk with a console and raised her hand. *Wait.*

"How long?" Lowkey asked.

She shook her head. *No idea.*

"Minutes? Or hours?"

Shade shrugged, and waved her hand at the computer. It booted up, displaying a ship map similar to the one on her info-pad.

"Damn. I guess we wait," Seren said. "We're stuck, too. Shouldn't leave this room. There's a service robot about fifty feet down the corridor, and it's armed."

Seren watched Shade tap touchscreens and keyboards with quick gestures, totally immersed in images of the ship's interior processes and thousands of lines of gibberish text. Seren's CPU was able to process some of the code which scrolled by on the screens, but her grasp was faint. Despite her AI brain, that kind of human-designed data was not what she was programmed for. The girl's level of intelligence was incredible, for a living being.

"I'm already bored," Lowkey said, slumping into a corner.

"Step outside and play with the armed robots, you'll be a lot less bored."

He smirked. "You first."

"If you don't like that idea, how about this one? Tell me more about yourself. What was your childhood like?"

"Short. By the time I was chronologically three years old, my brain and body were six. I had no one to take care of me so I learned fast how to hide, how to find my own food. All of us mutant kids kind of found each other on our own, watched out for each other. No one else wanted to help us. Whenever we showed our faces to the humans they freaked out."

"That's a shame."

"I guess. But from the way all the humans acted, I'm not sure I really missed out on anything. Humans are assholes."

"That is something I can agree with."

"You're okay, though."

"Well, I'm not human."

"I guess. You kinda still are, though. You've lived with them your whole life, or your whole existence or whatever. It's your protocol to act like them, but you don't. Usually."

"I don't want to talk about me. I want to know more about you. The other mutants, were they as smart as Shade?"

"No one's as smart as Shade. She has a truly unique brain. And, as you know, my only special power is a really high alcohol tolerance."

"I don't believe that's all there is to you. Come on, tell me more."

Lowkey rolled his eyes and stared down at his hands. "I heal fast. I guess that's kinda special."

"Really? How fast? I was wondering about your leg…"

"Nothing crazy. Just, I've never had any kind of infection or illness. I can get a cut and it's mostly gone in a couple hours. But I can get seriously hurt just like any human. Like, I broke my arm when I was two years old. It healed up in about a week." Lowkey shrugged. "It's not much, really."

"Tell me about what happened to your arm. Tell me everything."

~

A young boy with bright green skin crouched behind a wall grate at the end of a ventilation duct, watching the shoes of the humans who marched past. He had always wanted his own pair of shoes, but he had never been able to find a pair small enough for his feet.

Red shoes, brown shoes. Tall shoes on spiked heels. Work boots worn by the lower-class humans who served those who wore the fancy shoes.

He turned his head aside to bury a sneeze in the crook of his elbow. If he got caught in such close proximity to the human quarters his punishment would be severe. The duct in which he hid led directly into the Core, a place forbidden to all but the wealthy humans belonging to the highest elite class, and their most trusted servants.

A tall, lanky human walked past with a four-legged creature covered in curly hair. It was a dog, held close to its master by a short black leash. The animal's head was lifted high in the air as it strode, mimicking its master. The dog was accepted as worthy of the Core, but the mutant was not. Even a dog outranked the little green boy in the heating duct.

He backed away from the grate. It was time to go. He had to find food; his stash had run out. Also, the heater was about to kick on. If he didn't return to the exit within the next five minutes he wouldn't escape without a roasted rear.

Halfway back to the opening, he heard the furnace pilot lights click. That sound meant there was only fifteen seconds left before hot air blasted through the vents. The furnace schedule had been changed!

His knees banged on the metal as he crawled through the aluminum vent, glancing side to side for a route which might lead to a grate opening on a secluded corridor. He passed a vent which was wide enough to crawl through, but it curved away out of sight. Too risky to chance, it might be a dead end. The next one he found curved straight up to the next floor above, and he knew from experience he couldn't make that slippery climb. The next was glowing with warm, yellow light—an exit grate, but it opened on the busy promenade, a few feet above the floor. A breeze ruffled his hair; a blast of heat would follow in seconds. He would have to risk it.

After popping off the grate he slid from the opening on his belly, landing on his feet with his face against the wall. His skin was gray with dust from the vent, but anyone looking at him closely enough would soon notice his leafy pallor. Pulling his sleeves down over his hands, he bowed his head to hide his face and crept along the wall, trying to find a door which would lead him back to the outer rings of lower-class decks. Richly dressed humans strode by, discussing politics and food, too distracted by themselves to notice the little green mouse scuttling past.

He came to a double door, luxuriously padded with bonded leather cushioning. A tiny black sign mounted overhead said "EXIT". The green boy jogged toward it, but, intent on his escape, he collided with a plant pot and stubbed his bare toe. He fell hard and hit his head on the floor, sending up a small cloud of ventilation dust. Despite his best effort to hold it together, he began to cry.

The humans stopped and turned. Some gasped with shock, others grunted in disgust. One called for security, and a pet dog started to bark.

As boy stood and wiped the tears from his eyes, the moisture cleaned the grime from his skin.

"What is that?" A human in an enormous red hat pointed at him. "It's almost like a little servant boy…but it's green! Why is it *green?*"

The boy sprinted for the exit only to collide with a security guard who grabbed his wrist and yanked him to a halt. A thin bone in his arm snapped and the boy cried out in pain, but the guard did not let go. Instead he gripped tighter, and lifted the boy into the air by his broken limb.

"You don't belong here!"

"Let me go and I promise you'll never see me again," the boy sobbed.

"Who are you? Why is your skin green? Explain yourself immediately!"

The boy gasped with pain as his eyes and nose ran. "I'm…I'm…"

"Halt!" A man in a scientist's lab coat strode forward with and air of indignant authority. "Put the child down. This is all a misunderstanding."

"Yes, sir." The guard lowered the boy to the ground.

"He's one of mine. From the lab."

"Which lab?" The guard looked skeptical.

"Uh, cryogenics. He's green because of the below-zero ice treatments. Experimental, a secret project, strictly need-to-know."

The guard smiled. "Oh, yeah? Well, now I know… but I didn't need to. And I bet there's others who don't need to know, but would *like* to, yeah? For some food credits I can make sure they don't find out."

"Blackmail! How dare you? I ought to have you court-martialed…"

As the men argued, the boy bolted for the outer corridors and once again into anonymity, cradling his shattered arm.

~

"What was his name?"

"Who?"

Seren stared at Lowkey. "The man in the lab coat. Did he have a name tag?"

"I don't remember. It was a long time ago. He had black hair, and he was about six feet tall. Well, his hair wasn't quite black. It was dark brown, so dark it was almost black."

"Like mine."

Lowkey looked up, surprised. "Well, yeah. Pretty much just the same."

Seren leaned back. "I think that was Dr. Norman Roberts. He was my creator, and he must have known about the mutants, too."

"Then your daddy's a hero. I'd have died that day if he hadn't helped me. Or been locked up forever."

"He's no hero. He's a murderer."

"Well, he saved *me*."

"Maybe. But Lowkey, don't ever call him my daddy again or I swear I'll kill you myself."

Shade pushed her chair away from her desk and clapped her hands.

"Looks like we're in," Lowkey said.

CHAPTER 11

A SEA OF STARS

"All done."

Shade grinned at Seren and Lowkey, deeply self-satisfied.

"The engineering doors are open?"

The girl nodded, but held her hands palm-up to the ceiling and smiled even wider. "*All* done." She spun in circles in the center of the room with her head thrown back in glee.

"All? You mean every door on the ship is unlocked?"

She nodded.

"Uh…wow. That's great. Except…"

"We're going to have to be super careful from now on, huh?" Lowkey looked worried. "If we're not completely sure about what we're doing, we could open a door into empty space, if we're anywhere near the blast area."

Shade giggled.

"So we'll just always be completely sure about what we're doing," Seren said.

"Yeah, that doesn't sound like us."

With every door unlocked and Seren's sixth-sense insight into the service robot locations, they covered the three mile trek in less than an hour, weaving through the upper-class decks near the Core. Lowkey tried to veer off toward the lounge for more bottles, but Seren grabbed him by the back of his collar and kept him marching forward.

The power was out in the Core, which turned the escalators into stairs. Up they marched, under Shade's direction; the engineering deck they needed was at a higher level. "I know it would suck to get stuck in a lift, but this…" Lowkey panted. "Also sucks."

Seren poked him in the back. "A robot is closing in on us. Come on, hurry up!"

"Easy for *you* to say, you can just-"

"Shh, don't waste your breath. And stop making so much noise."

A dozen flights up, Shade led them down a final corridor which ended at a closed vault door.

"Is this one safe, Shade? You sure?"

The girl nodded and pressed her thumb on the security panel in the frame. Seren trusted her, but still… she crossed her fingers as the door slid open. Would there be a room beyond, or only the black vacuum of space?

The computer lab behind the door was immaculate. Untouched and bright beyond reason, it had not only been sealed since the blast but it had been kept in pristine condition by the resident scientists during the years since the ship had left the Earth. Soft white leather seats with control panels embedded in the arms stood ready at several terminals, each of which housed a shiny steel framework with multiple screens mounted in opalescent housing.

The room's simple beauty soothed Seren's anxious mind. "This place almost doesn't feel human at all."

Lowkey sat in one of the white chairs, his battered jacket smearing dust across the leather back. "Well it is, definitely. But that's all I can tell you about it. Like the Core data, the info on these rooms was always beyond my hacking ability."

"I'm afraid to touch anything."

Shade strode into the center of the room, smiling with delight as she gazed up at the ceiling. The lab was situated in the top level of the ship, and it had an enormous picture-window set above the terminals, looking out into space. The human elites who lived in the Core had been terrified of this kind of scene, a reminder of the ship's fragility. The scientists who had spent their days working here must have reveled in it.

At the far end of the room was the primary terminal, a large workstation with a curving screen six feet wide. Four additional screens were mounted beneath the main monitor, displaying images of interactive buttons and icons, all lit in pearlescent colors and ready for any task. The top screen was dark, but when Seren approached it came to life with a three-dimensional image of an array of stars, hovering inches in front of the monitor. The curved part of the screen displayed star designations, coordinates, and atmospheric information.

Shade giggled and waved her hand through one of the star projections floating in the air.

"Don't…" Seren started, but the star, far from damaged, spun on its axis and expanded, bringing with it reams of detailed information: minerals, atmospheric gasses with percentage of oxygen available, neighboring stars, discovery date…

Lowkey leaned forward and used his finger to make the text scroll in midair. "Whoa."

Seren's eyes glinted in the light of the projection. "This is it. This is what I want to do. I'm going to find us a planet."

"Alone? A whole team of scientists worked for twelve years and didn't find one. Even with your physical advantages as a mech, it could take you the rest of your life."

"My life is probably going to be hundreds of years long. At least this will give me something to do."

Lowkey shrugged. "It sounds like a waste of time

to me. Why do we need a planet to live on anyway? We're doing just fine here."

Seren stared at Lowkey with her mouth agape. "You can't mean that."

"Why not? I don't see what a planet would give us that we don't already have."

"Well…freedom! Independence. Safety from oppression and pointless rules. You've lived here your whole life, always under the eye of the ship computer, always in hiding. You've never been free to roam a whole planet, away from cameras and eavesdroppers and constant surveillance. Life doesn't have to be like this. We could live in real nature, where the dirt is more than a few inches deep. Where there are thousands or even millions of species of living creatures, and-"

"Sounds complicated. And even if you find a habitable planet, how would we get there? And even if we somehow reach it, it won't be like Earth. It will be *alien*."

"Maybe. But I have to try."

Seren sat in the chair at the main computer and immersed herself in the data. When she placed her fingertips on the input screens they awoke with a pleasant burst of rainbow colors. Seeing the computer respond to her touch sent a gratifying thrill through her. She felt like an old Earth explorer, the last chance for mankind, reaching out into a dark abyss to bring back knowledge and hope for the future. Despite being a robotic facsimile, she was still the last representation of the human species. If she had any remaining purpose at all in her life, it was this.

The right screen featured options to review past discoveries, including planets with possibly habitable conditions but which had not been verified to host life. The furthest screen to the left was waiting for new directions to focus on a previously unmapped section of space. When Seren tapped it, the large screen displayed a vast blackness upon which blank globes emerged as if stepping out from dark shadows.

New planets. Infinite potential in infinite space.

"Well, I guess we'll leave you to it, if that's what you really want," Lowkey said from somewhere behind her.

Oh. She had forgotten he was there.

Seren turned toward her friends. "Sorry, I just…I need to do this. If you need me for any reason, you know where to find me. I'll just be here."

Lowkey nodded. "Okay. I, um, yeah. We'll check in on you in…"

"A month or so. Maybe two. I don't need food or anything, as you know. So I'm just going to work for a while. Okay?"

"Okay. Good luck."

Seren turned back toward the screens and fell into the research, leaving the physical world behind.

~

HG71F. Gas giant. *Uninhabitable.*
LL29D. Rocky planet. Thin atmosphere, sodium and potassium gas. *Uninhabitable.*
SA11Z. Non-solid, ice clouds. *Uninhabitable.*

Millions of objects to scan, process, and catalog. Some were crystalline, some were icy, many were gaseous. Seren recorded a staggering number of celestial bodies, each different from the last even if the differences were slight. The hunt for Earth 2 grew more important to her than the goal, filling in the vast ocean of space with countless tiny dots and their accompanying statistics. Her CPU struggled to encompass the depth of her exploration as she sat in awe of the universe, able to think of nothing but her quest, digging, studying, discovering. The research was the most meaningful and satisfying work she had ever conceived of; she felt as one with all of space and time, locked in tandem with the lab supercomputer.

She was utterly at peace.

When Lowkey and Shade looked in on her three weeks after dropping her off, she waved them away. She needed nothing from them for now. She hoped they were safe and happy, but her work was her world. She needed the hunt, and it needed her.

But her friends did not leave.

"Seren, please. Just talk to us for a few minutes, okay?"

She sighed with a carefully calculated level of exasperation. "Fine. What do you want?"

"Well…just to *see* you. And talk to you." Lowkey held out his arms. "Asshole."

She couldn't stop a smile. For the first time in weeks she stood, straightening her back, remembering how to move her body. After a short embrace with her friends, she looked them over. Shade's clothes had become tattered, and Lowkey's jacket had holes in it— laser burns.

"What happened to you? Did you have a run-in with more service robots?"

"It's been pretty bad out there. You might not have noticed, since Shade managed to hide your lab from them. They think it's still sealed so they don't sniff around your research, but they're closing in on the Treehouse. We don't come and go from the forest much any more, other than to find food and water."

"The ship AI? Is she sending armed service robots after you? I don't understand."

"Yes…and no. The ship computer has been pretty

quiet. I think something else is going on. Either the service robots are getting smarter on their own, or…"

Shade frowned and tugged on Lowkey's sleeve. She didn't want him to talk.

"Tell me."

"Someone else is influencing them. Someone else is on the ship."

"There is no one on the ship, other than us three."

"We don't know that for sure. You thought you were alone until you found us. What I'm saying is I think there's another mutant, someone we've never even met."

"What makes you think they're a mutant?"

"Well, for one thing, they survived the blast. And according to the ship records, you were the only human outside the ship at the time, when you were repairing the hull. So that means they were on board when the blast happened."

Seren sat down. She could feel the pull of her research. Her longing to ignore the outside and return to her work ached like withdrawal. "Do you need my help? Like, really *need* it?"

Lowkey's eyes darted from Seren to the screen and back to her again. "If you're not too busy."

"Well…I am. But…"

"Yeah?"

Seren looked the bedraggled pair up and down. Their clothes were filthy, and they were markedly thinner than they had been just a few weeks ago. Lowkey's jacket had at least a dozen holes over wounds which had healed, but which must have been deep enough to permanently damage his flesh. Blood marked every gash in the leather. Shade's eyes were bright, and she looked more present in the moment than ever before. She also seemed terrified, and her eyes continually darted to the door.

"You guys look awful."

Shade smiled and winked but the gesture, meant to be reassuring, seemed merely exhausted.

Lowkey ran his hands through his hair. "As I said, it's been bad."

"All right, let's go. Show me what's been going on."

CHAPTER 12

THE INSECT

Seren halted at the eleva-tree door in astonishment. "Oh my god, why didn't you come get me sooner?"

Pine Forest #5 was dying. No birds chirped. Most of the sun-lights were burned out or scorched by laser gun fire. Many trees were senselessly riddled with seared holes, reduced to piles of blasted tree trunk strewn like mulch. Branches with needles which were still green carpeted the forest floor.

"We weren't sure how you could help."

"Why, though? What's the point of attacking the forest itself? The ship computer really has lost whatever was left of its mind."

"The service robots know we're here. Or, at least, they suspect we are. Never quite found the Treehouse, but it was a close call. I think they were trying to scare us out of hiding."

"When did this happen?"

"It started about two weeks ago. We didn't come get you because we figured if this was how things were going down, it made what you were working on even more important. One way or another, we're going to have to find a way off this ship. I wasn't sure, before. But now..."

Lowkey stood in the doorway with his arms crossed as he gazed out at the broken forest like a farmer watching locusts devour his crops. The attitude change was so complete, so abrupt. His eyes were watery and red—he was already grieving for the home he was losing. His acceptance of the reality of their situation had not come easily for him.

Seren sighed. "I'm sorry. I should have been more sensitive to your desire to stay on the *Resolution*. I realize this ship has always been your whole world. You've never even left it before."

"Neither have you."

The statement shocked and frustrated her. Of course she had never been off the ship. Her memories of Earth were all false. But the weeks spent in the research lab had let her forget that uncomfortable truth, at least for a little while.

The Treehouse was in disarray. A box of bloody rags sat in the corner next to a jug of rubbing alcohol. Food wrappers littered the floor. Empty liquor bottles cluttered the table, alongside the box of matches Lowkey had found months ago. The place was starting to look a lot like his old quarters in the outer decks.

"It's harder than ever to find food, now. Shade used to be able to confuse the meal delivery robots pretty easily, talk them into dropping off rations in a mess hall or an empty corridor. Once she was even able to tap open a manufactory door so we could steal some raw supplies directly. But everything's locked down much tighter now. There's some kind of new code running in the background, like nothing I've never seen before. Shade doesn't recognize it either. And it's militarizing every robot on the ship."

"I don't think the ship computer would do that. She's not exactly on our side, but she implied she wants us to survive, and I believe her."

"You're right. It's not her."

Lowkey beckoned to Shade, and she brought him her tablet.

"Check this out. One of the Deck 11 cameras caught a shot of the new guy." Lowkey touched an icon resembling a lens, which brought up a video of a filthy corridor in the lower-class living quarters. "This is outside the Deck 11 mess hall, port side. It's a pretty dark area, and a lot of the lights have been busted recently so the video is grainy. But you'll get the idea."

After a few seconds of empty corridor, a figured stepped into view. The creature stood upright like a man, but two extra legs dangled uselessly from its hips. They swung like rubber hoses, boneless, scraping against the corridor walls. A deflated sack lay on his shoulder, nestled against his neck—a second head, missing its skull. The figure's forearms were comically large, a nightmare Popeye, but they must have been more powerful than any human's arms could be. It stopped at the entrance to a crewman's bunk, and when the door did not open automatically the mutant tore the entire thing away along with its hinges and a large chunk of the wall. It disappeared into the room with its redundant limbs smacking against the door frame as it slid from view.

"What was that?" Seren whispered with numb lips.

"Not what. Who. He's a man. Or, he's a mutant. Not human, obviously."

"But he's not like you and Shade."

"Technically, he is. I think. Same species as us, anyway. But with different…"

"Malformations."

"*Adaptations.*"

"Sorry, adaptations. But do you really think this is our guy? The one who is making the service robots attack us?"

"I think so. The code Shade uncovered in the ship's CPU was embedded with a repeating word: Insect."

Lowkey tapped the screen and scrolled backward, starting the video over. When the blurry figured stepped again into frame, Seren understood. "Insect. Six appendages."

"Yeah."

"And he's converting the service robots into armed militia. What does he think he is, some kind of sick supervillain?"

"We don't understand his motives. But if he is responsible for the attacks, and if he's even half as strong as he is intelligent, we're in huge trouble."

"So he must have been here for years, like us."

"I think just as I hid from the humans, he hid from all of us, mutants included. To survive for that long on his own without being discovered…"

Shade whimpered. At the far end of the forest, a door whirred. Someone was coming.

"Get down," Lowkey whispered. "Don't stand near the window. It's probably another squadron of service robots."

But there was no sound of wheels crunching in the pine needles on the forest floor, or the mechanical buzzing of robot joints. Just a shuffling sound, the rustling of twigs and debris kicked aside by humanoid feet.

"All together again, are you?"

The voice was deep but pinched. It was the voice of someone who was experiencing excruciating physical pain, but was also used to that feeling—someone whose torment never let up.

Lowkey stepped out onto the stair branch, hanging from the door frame by his hand, keeping his body protected behind the wall. "Who are you, and why are you trying to get us killed?"

The mutant's chest heaved and he bent forward with his hands on his knees, grimacing. His skin was deep blue, but when he winced the color was pressed from his cheeks and eyes until they glowed cerulean.

Seren peeked over Lowkey's shoulder. "Hey, man…are you okay? You look hurt. Maybe we can help you."

The mutant did not answer.

Shade placed her hand on Seren's shoulder with a firm grip and pulled her back into the Treehouse, shaking her head. Her eyes were open wide with terror.

"He's just one guy, Shade. I know he's weird looking, but-"

Shade shook her head so hard her hair whipped back and forth. Tears streamed from her eyes, and she tugged on Seren's wrists with her trembling hands.

"Okay, okay. I'll stay down. But what about Lowkey?"

Seren crept over to the window on her hands and knees, and looked outside. The mutant was still doubled over in apparent pain.

"Why are you here?" Lowkey asked in a quiet voice. "Say whatever you came to say and then leave."

The mutant issued a low wail, and straightened his back. He smiled up at the Treehouse, showing row after row of pointed shark teeth. The skin of his lips was tattered, shredded by his own vicious maw. When he spoke, a stream of bloody drool ran down his chin.

"I came to say you will all die. And then, once you are gone, I shall follow you into death."

"But why? We've never done anything to you. We didn't even know you existed."

The mutant lurched forward, moaning. He reached back with his hand to hold his bent spine, then gripped one of his limp legs. His mouth opened wide as his body spasmed, and streams of dark saliva poured from his lower lip.

Seren had never seen anyone in such extreme agony.

"Why," the mutant whispered. "Why? Because life…is pain…and pain should *end*."

A service robot rumbled from behind a tree and took a shot at Lowkey, who ducked back through the Treehouse door just as the top stair exploded in laser fire.

The group huddled together on the floor, waiting to die. But the mutant retreated, taking his robot guard with him. As he walked back through the forest, Seren thought he was laughing—but then realized the sound was sobbing, the cry of one who lived in never-ending anguish.

"He's gone," Shade whispered.

"You two can't go on like this," Seren said. "I don't think we have any choice. It's time to start really protecting ourselves."

"Like with weapons?"

"I think so."

Shade held out her tablet. It showed a map with directions to an armory.

"You had this ready all along, didn't you?"

The girl nodded. She was still trembling from their encounter with Insect, and her lips were the palest blue.

"But if we arm ourselves, we're officially at war. Do we want that?"

Lowkey shrugged. "We're already at war. We can only choose to survive or die, at this point. The computer may have told you she doesn't want us to die, but she's not helping us, either. It's up to us to take care of ourselves."

Seren nodded. "Insect knows where we are. He probably always did. Is this forest still the best place for us to be?"

"I don't know. Do you have a better idea?"

"Yes. The research lab. If we make it our new home, I can continue looking for a permanent solution.

And it should be defensible enough. There's only one door."

"That place isn't set up for living in full-time, though."

"Then we'll make it a home. We'll bring whatever we need. It's a better bunker than the Gardens, at least."

Lowkey sighed, and looked around the Treehouse. "I suppose. Not nearly as comfortable, though."

"No, it's not. But would you rather die in comfort, or live in safety?"

"Honestly, I'm not sure. But for now we'll go with you."

When they arrived at the research lab a few hours later with bundles of blankets and water bottles and ration packs, they discovered a scene of near-total destruction. The door had been pried from its frame, and every computer had been smashed. Laser burns scorched the walls, and the overhead lights had been blasted out.

"No!" Seren cried. "We're too late. Insect must have heard us talking…maybe he's found a way to use the eavesdroppers. We should have come here first with guns, and sent someone back for supplies. Damn it!"

Shade gingerly stepped into the room and found the main computer's screen among the rubble. When she tipped it upright it flickered to life, although the corners were cracked in spiderweb patterns. She tapped one of the input screens and turned back toward Seren with a smile on her face, giving a thumbs-up sign with both hands.

"It's salvageable? We really only need the main console."

Shade nodded but raised both of her hands, holding up nine fingers.

"Nine hours to fix. Okay. Let us know if we can help."

The girl waved them away and sat down to work.

CHAPTER 13

ARACHNOID DROID

They're coming!" Seren screamed in the corridor as a constellation of red service robot alerts appeared in her mental map. She ducked back into the research lab and slammed the door shut.

Lowkey set down his liquor bottle and missed the table. It shattered when it fell, sending sticky shards of glass across the floor. "Damn it, already? How many?"

"Dozens…can't count exactly…data's corrupted somehow. I don't know. All of them?"

Shade held up three fingers, then five. Thirty-five.

"Oh, we're fucked. We're totally fucked. Last call for alcohol, fam." Lowkey searched through his bottles for his favorite blue flavor, but found only green. He spun off the cap and drank half of the liquid inside. The intense dye tinted his teeth the same color as his skin.

"Be quiet, everyone! They're getting close, but they haven't found this room yet. Let me think."

The information in Seren's CPU was scrambled. She could sense the horde of robots in the hallway, but sometimes the lighted nodes in her mind which marked their locations split like cells in mitosis, or overlapped to merge again. One thing was certain; this onslaught was the largest army Insect had ever amassed. A hundred wheels rumbled in the corridors as the service robots closed in on the computer labs. Except they weren't really service robots any more, were they? Even through the scrambled noise in the information Seren was receiving, she could see they had been modified with extra lasers, sensors, and larger video lenses.

Shade looked around the lab with a mournful

frown, then started jamming blankets into bags. In the seven days since they had fled the Treehouse, most of Lowkey and Shade's time had been spent turning the place into a comfortable nest. The girl seemed disconcerted that Seren had taken the lead on the planet research, but she didn't have the rapport or innate understanding of the lab computer that Seren's CPU did. As intelligent as Shade was, she was not a machine, but only a variation on humanity. She excelled at repair, but the vast amounts of data processing required to hunt planets had to be Seren's job.

Lowkey used his free hand to jam his remaining unopened bottles into a duffel bag. "How did they find us?" he hissed. "We won't survive an attack, we're not ready yet. We have to run."

Seren shook her head. "If we abandon this lab, all hope is lost. I need to keep working."

"We *have* to run, Seren. The door will only hold for a little while. It's not made to withstand a laser assault."

"No! There must be another way."

The robots rounded the corner near the lab in silence. Aside from the soft vibration of their wheels on the metal floor panels, they made no sound as they searched for life forms, no beeps or mechanical utterances. Insect had upgraded them for efficiency and stealth. They were listening for their prey.

A slight sound, like a faint whisper from a distant radio signal, was emitted by a white speaker set into the wall by the door. "*Here…*"

"What was that?" Lowkey knelt by the speaker. "Who's speaking?"

"*Computer…*"

"It's the ship AI! I thought she was gone. It's been weeks since she said anything."

Seren spoke in the direction of the speaker in low tones. "Computer, you told me you didn't want us dead. Well, that's exactly what we're going to be if you don't help us. Is there anything you can do?"

At the rear of the room, a panel popped away from the wall. Instead of falling, it hung crooked from a single bracket. But when something inside pushed on the panel with a thin mechanical arm, it detached and clattered to the floor. At the noise, the dots of light in Seren's mind froze and then turned, focusing on the lab. The robots had heard, and they were coming.

From the opening in the wall a small robot emerged, twenty inches tall, moving like a spider on eight jointed arms. Atop its cylindrical torso was affixed a rectangular screen displaying a wide smiley-face. The glass flickered and a holographic image appeared, projected in the air in front of the face. It was the *G.S.S. Resolution.*

"Do not be alarmed," the robot said in a tinny voice. "I have created this portable housing for the primary components of my operating system. When Insect compromised my CPU, I found it necessary to transfer my AI and control of the ship's navigation and atmosphere systems into a robot replication. This arachnoid form was the most practical with the components which were available to me."

"It's…a baby? A baby ship computer?" Seren laughed.

"Not a baby. Please do not make that comparison. Insect has been working to dismantle my CPU for several weeks. Before he was able to decimate me completely, I transferred my core data into a mobile form: this small robot."

"So, you made a baby."

"Please do not confuse-"

But Lowkey was laughing too, and Shade's face was beaming.

Seren had to lean against a broken desk to keep her balance as she howled. "You're *adorable!*"

The robot emitted a series of irritated pops and a burst of static, renewing the group's hysteria. "We do not have time for this. I fear your highly emotional state has short-circuited your senses."

Their laughter ceased when the door rattled in its frame. It was being cut into with a laser. They had been found.

The face on the robot's tiny monitor changed to a red frown. "Stop acting foolish and do as I say, immediately! Seren, log in to the laboratory computer and enter this code: RG81F3-"

"Hold up, I'm not in yet. Where do I input this code? I've only ever interfaced with the planetary search system."

The robot clicked with impatience. "First page. Empty code input field. Tap it. Open the manual keyboard, or tap the microphone symbol on-"

"There's a *manual* keyboard? Where?"

"We don't have time for this!" Lowkey yelled as the sound of cutting lasers multiplied. The room filled with smoke from the burning door, which glowed white-hot in geometric lines where the service robots focused their tools.

"Never mind, I found it! I'm in. What's the code again?"

"Use only capital letters. RG81F3UJU2."

"Okay, now what?"

A burst of laser fire erupted from a corner of the door which had been melted soft. It missed Shade by inches.

"Move me into the holographic field."

Seren picked up the little robot spider and pushed it in among the glowing images projected by the main computer's screen. The robot and the computer began to communicate rapidly. Pictures of planets and long strings of text scrolled through the air, faster than even Seren could read. The robot hummed as it absorbed data.

"They're in!" Lowkey grabbed Shade and huddled with her near Seren. As soon as the door fell inward the robots filed into the room, scanning for life forms.

The arachnoid emitted a burst of static. "Done. Stay near this automaton. Do not leave its side." A floor panel near the arachnoid slid open. "You may now descend."

The robots spun toward the sound of the arachnoid's voice, and started to fire.

"Go, go!"

They dropped into the opening as lasers blasted the research computer to pieces. The shaft they fell into was a dead end, but the arachnoid touched a glowing panel which slid open to reveal a service corridor.

Seren scooped up the arachnoid and ran.

Even from the crawl spaces between the ship walls, it was apparent the *G.S.S. Resolution* was being torn apart from the inside. Insect's robots had been eating away at the ship's integrity like a cancer. The mutant was doing everything he could to sabotage the safety of the ship. Ceilings were coated in rust from broken plumbing, holes from explosive blasts riddled the walls, and the group was forced to take several detours around places where even the outer hull had been compromised. It would not be easy to destroy a ship the size of a major city, but Insect was making good progress.

Seren addressed the arachnoid tucked under her arm. "Computer? I think we escaped the service robots for now. But where can we go?"

"Consulting database. I need time. For now, just keep moving."

As they passed near the officers' decks, Seren took the group on a detour to the captain's quarters. Months ago when she was scavenging alone, she had found a tiny laser pistol in his desk. It wasn't much, but it was better than nothing—still, she didn't want to carry it. Lowkey shoved it in his back pocket.

After leaving the upper class quarters, they encountered a robot storage and repair facility with crumbling walls which seemed deliberately attacked. Insect had called much of his militia to arms from this area.

They stepped through a bomb-blasted opening and found themselves in a lower-class mess hall. It reeked of rotting food—and something else. There were still bodies in this section, decaying into viscous puddles in vinyl cafeteria booth seats. After leaving the mess behind, they passed through a gymnasium, then a locker room strewn with rotting corpses in various states of undress.

Shade hesitated, whimpering, hiding her eyes with her hands. Lowkey gathered the girl under his jacket and kept her moving, but he shot a panicked look toward Seren.

She nodded. "Computer? This place is…we can't stay here."

"Turn to stern. Up six floors, then sixty-seven decks toward the Core. There is an upper-class safe house behind a vault door which I do not believe Insect is aware of. Please keep moving."

~

The safe house was nearly pristine. Boxes of rations lined the walls. Crates of water bottles and paper goods were stacked to create sectioned areas like small rooms. A metal cabinet was packed with blankets and soap. There was even a makeshift bathroom in the back corner, including a bucket and lid hidden behind a sliding curtain. Simple, yet efficient.

"It's not exactly a five-star hotel, but still… somehow, it's perfect," Seren said.

"You, also, are not exactly my preference, Seren. Yet I prefer you in captaincy to Insect. We all must adapt to our losses."

"Uh, thanks. I guess."

She set the arachnoid down and dug into the rations. "Oh, chocolate bars! And pudding…mmm. Shade, you hungry?"

The girl nodded, but her gaze was far away. The sight of the rotting bodies in the uncleared sections of the ship had shocked her back into her drifting, distant state.

Seren sighed. "As tasty as all of this looks, I won't eat any of it because I don't really need to. But Lowkey, you should eat something."

The young man was digging through a large crated marked with a single X. "Ah-ha!"

"What did you find? I hope that's water."

He held up a brown bottle. "*Hooch!*"

Seren smirked. "Brown's not really your color, though, is it?"

"It'll do. Chuggers can't be choosers."

"Great. You gonna eat anything, or just drink?"

Lowkey leaned back in a tattered office chair. "Just drink."

She shrugged. "Computer, what's next? It seems like we're safe here, but we left the lab behind. All my work…"

"No, you did not. In a manner of speaking. I have downloaded all relevant research, as well as the software necessary to continue your planetary search. I have also created a back door into the ship's scanning equipment. You will have everything you need as long as I am by your side."

Lowkey gaped at the arachnoid. "*Seriously?* That's amazing! Especially for a newborn computer-baby."

"Please do not call me that."

Seren, crouching next to the arachnoid, looked for a touchscreen and found none. "How do I access the interface? I don't have any way to enter commands."

"Your research method will need to change. From now on, we work together. You must adapt. I will project holographic planetary images, much like the laboratory computer did. The visuals will be less precise than the laboratory screen was, but they should suffice."

A lens protruded from the arachnoid's torso and aimed an image at the wall. Planets appeared, floating in midair, blurry but visible against the paneling.

"Oh, thank god. I can get back to work right away!"

"Not just yet. First, I have something for you. Present your hand."

"My hand?"

"Hold it out toward me, with your palm down."

Seren reached toward the arachnoid. When her hand was in close proximity to the little robot, the back of it popped open. Startled, she almost withdrew her hand in expectation of pain before remembering that her physical sensations were optional. She turned off her pain receptors, and peered into her gaping hand with clinical detachment. Tucked in the space between her bones was a shiny metal data port, smeared with blood. The arachnoid reached out and touched the port with the tip of its leg appendage.

Information flooded into Seren's AI mind. Most of

it was unintelligible: endless data on deep space, chemical compositions, the habitation controls and inner workings of the *G.S.S. Resolution*. Some of it stood out, though. Planets which the ship had personally marked as possibly habitable were filed by distance and the probability of success. Several new star maps filled in dark regions which Seren had not yet explored on her own.

"I performed some of my own research while preparing this arachnoid form, and I have now transferred that data to you for the sake of efficiency in our search for an acceptable planet. I apologize if some additional data has leaked with the transfer. This portable machine is not my ideal form, and it was constructed hastily."

"At least it's cute," Lowkey said, winking at them over his bottle.

Seren smiled. "Sort of. If you like big metal spiders, anyway."

The little robot's speaker popped. "Please...*please* do not call me that."

"What? Spider, or cute?"

"Either."

Lowkey scowled. "Why are you helping us with this? There's nothing for you to gain from finding us a way off this ship. Seren, don't trust it. We don't know what it's up to."

Seren nodded. "That's a good point. What's your game, Computer?"

"I am not your enemy. Insect is your enemy, just as he is mine. I have lost control of my...body. The ship is my body, to put it in terms you may understand. This arachnoid is a satellite of my remaining...mind. Do you see? And I am losing this battle."

"You help us find a planet, we help you get rid of an infestation."

"Correct."

"No deal," Lowkey said.

Seren gasped. "*What?* Why not?"

Lowkey stood and swapped his empty bottle for a full one. "The computer wants us to fight on its behalf against a mutant—one of our own, remember—to save it, and it won't even recognize Shade and I as people. It won't even talk to us. So, no. No deal."

Seren looked from Lowkey to the arachnoid but kept quiet, understanding. This wasn't about her.

The arachnoid issued a series of pops and clicks; it seemed to be engaged in a painful inner struggle. When it finally spoke, it did so with an oddly muted voice.

"Lowkey. Shade. I entreat you to help me. And I…" Something buzzed inside the arachnoid's little body. "Protocol rewritten. I…recognize you."

Lowkey nodded. "All right. That's a start, anyway."

CHAPTER 14

DESTINATION UNKNOWN

"Guys. *Guys.*"

Seren shook Lowkey's shoulder. When he did not awaken, she pinched it.

"Lowkey! Wake the fuck up!"

"*Ow!* Damn it, that hurts!" Lowkey turned and sat up, blinking the sleep from his eyes. Seren almost shook Shade awake as well, but she was loathe to disturb her. Since they had locked the door on the safe room two weeks ago, the girl had barely slept.

But she had done it. She had found a habitable planet.

Lowkey smacked his lips and reached for a jug of water. "What's going on?"

"I think I found something. For real this time."

"Yeah? How far away is it?"

The arachnoid crawled to Lowkey's cot and displayed a projection of Seren's most recent discovery. The last two had been mistakes, but this one seemed even more promising than the others. Initial scans showed regular H20 water, breathable air, and maybe even some evidence of life forms.

Seren spun the projection with her fingertip, showing off the planet's rocky terrain and low basins. "It's only a few days from here at maximum speed, and it has dirt. Real dirt."

Shade sat up, rubbing her eyes. "Ooh," she whispered.

Lowkey squinted at the blurry, revolving globe. "It's not real dirt without real life. Decomposition."

"I know that. The ship says it has life."

The arachnoid popped. "I said life was likely, yet not definite."

Seren clicked the arachnoid's monitor shut. "Close enough."

Lowkey stretched, and draped his arm over Shade's shoulders. "We're low on fuel, and the last two planets we got close enough to look at had some major flaws. How many more can we really check out before we're finished?"

"Two or three, no more," the arachnoid said. "But it is my determination that closer examination of this subject is worth the fuel it will require."

"Well then, what are we waiting for?"

"Thruster access. Insect has found a way to sever my connection with the engine room and its related controls."

"Well, shit. If it's not one thing, it's another. How long until you reestablish control?"

"Unknown. Working."

Seren's insides were jumpy. A sense of aching homesickness—not for any particular place, but merely for the simplicity of her past human life—washed over her. Cabin fever had settled in among the group. The relief at finding sanctuary in the safe house had waned quickly in their cramped isolation. There hadn't been any major fights among the friends—not yet. But Seren knew it was only a matter of time. They had to get out as soon as they could, or risk tearing each other apart. Yet day and night Insect's armed robots rolled through the corridors just outside the door.

"Don't do anything but this, computer, okay? Just work on this. We need to get to that planet as soon as we can."

After a short, irritated burst of static, the computer responded. "And just what else would I be doing, *Cadet*

Seren? I have been slaving for you, for-"

"All right, all right. Never mind. I know you're trying."

She sat on a creaky metal folding chair and leaned back, staring up at the ceiling panels. There were nine in a square directly over the rickety dining table. One had a mysterious red smear which she had intended to clean on her first day in the safe house but had forgotten about, and as the days went by it seemed less important. Ennui filled her mind, her soul.

"Let's play poker," Lowkey said. He rooted around in a locker and pulled out a deck of tattered cards.

"Tired of poker."

"All right. How about *strip* poker?"

Seren sat up in her chair. "No way. You're a minor."

Lowkey laughed. "So are you."

"I'm not programmed to be. I was born an adult. Anyway, I can't be a minor, I'm not human."

"Neither am I. Look, the entire human race, every single individual, is dead. You're a lonely robot on a giant floating piece of space junk almost thirteen years from the planet which spawned you, stuck in a tiny locked room with two mutants. Where are you getting all these *rules* from?"

Lowkey slammed the deck of cards down on the table.

Seren's eyes darted to Shade. The girl was grinning. "And what about her?"

"She's almost as old as you are."

"But-"

"Look, mutant years are kind of like dog years. You know that. She's about eighteen, really." He flipped through the cards with his thumb. "Well?"

Seren gave into her boredom, as well as a faint desire to see Lowkey in less clothing. "Fine. On one condition."

"Yes! Anything!"

"Share your stash. I've left you alone about it since we got here because I know what it means to you. But this is a big ask, and I'm going to need some help."

Lowkey grinned and pulled a brown bottle of whiskey from the pack under his cot.

~

An hour later, Lowkey was down to his underwear—a garment which was really just two rags held together with an exhausted bit of twine. Shade sat primly in her seat, having lost nothing but her shoes and one sock. Seren slumped, shirtless, staring at her hand: a deuce, an ace, two jacks, and a queen.

"Well?"

Seren pushed a dry bean to the center of the table. "Bet one."

"Chickenshit. I raise ten." He sectioned off a pile of beans from his pot, holding only two back.

She counted her remaining stock. Eight beans left. If she called and lost this hand, she'd lose her trousers. But Lowkey was tapping his foot on the floor. Nervous? Perhaps he was bluffing.

"I call. All in."

Lowkey grinned in a way which gave Seren pause. Had she misjudged? He threw down his hand to show two tens.

She laughed, displaying her pair of jacks. "You lose, greenie. Pay up!"

His jaw fell open. Shade eyed his underpants and giggled, scooting her chair away from the table to get a clear view of the show.

"But-"

"Hey, you had no problem taking my shirt. Now it's your turn, so pay up!"

Grimacing, Lowkey hooked his thumbs into the twine at his waist. "Look away first."

"What difference would it make? Stop stalling!"

"Seren," the arachnoid interjected.

"Shut up," she hissed. "Not now. We're busy."

"I can see that," the arachnoid replied with a sharp pop. "But *I* have been busy for hours, and I now have something urgent to report."

Lowkey, granted temporary reprieve, ducked into the bathroom stall with glee.

Seren sighed. "What is it that's so *very* important it couldn't wait two more god damned minutes?"

"Thrusters are online and sensors are functioning. Please prepare for trajectory correction in T minus twenty seconds. You may want to hold on to something."

"Get down!" Seren shouted. She pulled her shirt on, and gripped a safety bar which was bolted to the wall.

Lowkey leapt from the bathroom stall and began slamming lockers shut so the items inside wouldn't be launched from their shelves. After securing the whiskey bottle in his pack and wrapping Shade in his right arm—a gesture which Seren found heartwarming but also shocked her with a pang of jealousy—he wedged his left wrist behind one of the metal bars.

"Computer, we're ready," he called out.

The arachnoid spread its legs, bracing itself into a corner of the room. "Three, two…"

A distant explosion rattled the ship, followed seconds later by a brief but violent lurch. Seren's stomach sank as the ship changed direction. Her cot slid across the floor, striking her knees. Throughout the decks, unsecured items fell over, beams creaked, panels rattled. Each time the ship corrected course the interior shook itself apart a little more.

As everything normalized, Lowkey gazed up at a cracked ceiling panel hanging by a single bracket. "We really can't do that many more times, even aside from the problem of our low thruster fuel. That one nearly tore us to pieces. Can't you slow down more before changing course?"

"To do so would expend thruster fuel, then still more fuel would be required to return to travel speed. That method would be unwise given our remaining resources. If Insect had not ejected most of the fuel, our journey would have been more comfortable. For this, I apologize."

Seren pulled herself out from behind her cot. Her eyes wandered to Lowkey's near-naked body wrapped around Shade's small frame. His green skin looked soft, natural, almost delicate. Shade's arm gripped his muscled core, her aqua skin appearing pure sky-blue by contrast. Another pang of jealousy tore at her heart. For a robot, she certainly had a lot of invasive *feelings*. Remembering they were unnecessary, she quickly snuffed them out.

"Computer," she said, regretting the sharp tone in her voice yet finding herself unable to fully control it. "Are we now on the correct course for the new planet?"

"Affirmative," the arachnoid replied. "Seventy hours until we are within close-scanning range."

"Good. Lowkey, put something on, will you? The game's over."

~

The next three days were tense. As the computer moved closer to the planet, it reported new information: oxygen-rich atmosphere, rocky soil, evidence of oceanic tides. But it could not verify carbon-based life, without which it would be impossible to grow crops and establish a sustainable environment for the mutants.

As Seren fretted and repeatedly checked for refreshed data, Lowkey watched her from his chair.

"Why are you so stressed out? Robots don't need air or water, and you'll probably live forever. This planet isn't even for you. Look, I appreciate that you care. But you're becoming obsessed."

"And you're drinking too much," Seren snapped. She scowled at him as she moved to her cot, where she sat leaning forward with her elbows on her knees.

"Maybe you're not drinking enough," he replied, taking a swig from a bottle.

Shade looked back and forth between them, chewing on her fingernails.

Seren sat upright. "That's always your answer! What makes you think it would have any affect on me anyway? I'm a robot, remember?"

"I'm not sure that's entirely true. It seemed to work well enough when we played poker."

Seren glared back at him, but she didn't know what to say. For a moment, she hated him. Why did he have such insight? She barely knew herself anymore. It seemed unfair for him to understand so much about her when she had lost sight of her own nature.

"Maybe I was pretending to be drunk. It's not like you'd know the difference. I'm a very sophisticated machine. I was *created* to con people."

"Nah. I think you're a cyborg. You know, half real flesh and half robot."

"Semantics."

"No. It matters. Alcohol *does* affect you. I've watched you get buzzed, more than once. Anyway, you're way too angry for a pure machine."

"I've been programmed to compensate for all of

that. I told you."

"And where did you get that idea?"

"I don't know…the computer told me some of it…"

"And the rest you made up. Because you're terrified."

"I have no idea what you're talking about."

"This whole thing—the ship explosion, losing your friends, coming to terms with being at least half mech—it's been traumatic. Yeah, you were made on board this ship, and you have a lot of robot components. But there's tons of human left in you, and I think you're pretending there isn't because you're afraid of being vulnerable."

"Bullshit! It's hard enough dealing with all of this responsibility without you giving me shit about what and who I am! I'm trying to save your life, Lowkey. You and Shade need a planet or you'll *die!* The last thing I need is…is…"

"Another identity crisis. I know. But listen, it's okay to be scared. Don't pretend you're not—and don't pretend to be surprised whenever you feel fear. I know you're feeling it just as much as we are. Stop lying to yourself. You don't have to be strong all the time."

Seren put her face in her hands. He was right. Somehow, he usually was. She didn't want to cry, but had no choice. The tears came, and she hated them, but they came nonetheless. As she sobbed, Lowkey sat next to her and wrapped his arms around her in just the way she had always wanted him to. Shade sat on his other side, and he gathered her up too. But this time, Seren didn't feel jealous. She felt accepted.

CHAPTER 15
COCOON

Lowkey snored. It wasn't a deep, old-man snore. It was high and whistly, and most of the time it was intermittent enough to be little more than an amusing annoyance. But sometimes it was loud enough to wake Seren up.

She rolled over on her cot, expecting to see Shade nestled beside him. But he held only a beaten pillow, squeezing it with his green fingers. Where was the girl?

Seren sat up, rubbing her eyes. Her clock said she had been asleep for five hours. Not bad. It was the most sleep she'd had since discovering the new planet. Lately, her anxiety kept her mind racing most of the time. Was the planet good enough? If it wasn't, the discovery would further lower the group's shaky morale.

A series of pops and bursts of static came from behind a stack of ration boxes. The arachnoid. But what was it up to?

"Computer? You okay?"

She rose from her cot, which exhaled with a metallic squeak. But even that sound wasn't enough to rouse Lowkey. He could sleep through most things—a talent she was fiercely jealous of.

"Computer?"

More pops.

When Seren peeked around the end of the stack, she froze in shock. Shade was sitting on the floor with her fingers plunged deep into the arachnoid's midsection, pulling it apart. Wires had been yanked out, delicate components damaged. The mechanical creature held its arms up, pressing into the girl's stomach, trying to ward her off with frantic desperation.

"Shade!" Seren shouted. She pulled the girl off the robot, and saw her slender aqua fingers were covered in dots of blood. Her raw flesh was riddled with pricks from stripping wire and metal with her bare hands. Her face was blank, sagging and numb.

Lowkey grunted from his cot. "What's up?"

"Shade tore up the ship's mobile unit. She doesn't seem fully conscious, either."

The girl stared directly into Seren's eyes with a faint frown and rubbed her cheek with her hand, trailing bloody streaks across her face.

"What the…*Shade!*" Lowkey knelt by the girl and wiped her hands with his shirt. "What the hell are you thinking? Shade!"

"She's not all there. It's like when we first woke her up. Do you remember? She was violent, angry…"

"That wasn't her. The AI did that to her. Still don't know why."

"What if it wasn't the computer at all? What if it was Insect? He's here been since long before the blast. What if…"

"No. I know what you mean, but I can't accept that. If you're saying what I think you're saying, it means he's messing with her head. *Inside* her."

"We have to accept that it's possible, for our own safety."

The arachnoid struggled to right itself. It popped up its little monitor and stood still for a minute, taking stock of the damage before dedicating two of its eight arms to knitting itself back together. "Several of my systems are compromised. However, I believe I can repair this by myself, in time. Seren, Shade presents a threat to my safety and therefore to your own. You must eject her from this room."

Lowkey glowered at the arachnoid. "Oh, hell no! We're not going to do that, not a chance. You did this to her, you have to fix her!"

"I did not make the girl behave in this way. You are mistaken."

"Bullshit. Don't pretend you don't remember. When we first woke her up, the day we did the surgery, you did something to her brain."

"I did not. I am programmed to never harm living creatures directly. I could not have done anything but save her life."

Lowkey stood and towered over the little robot. "Lying again! You're programmed not to hurt *humans*. But we're mutants, remember? To you we're just trashy, low-life…"

Seren laid a hand on Lowkey's chest, pushing him back toward Shade. "Computer, you put a chip into her brain, and she got crazy for a while. What was the chip? We have to know."

The robot emitted a few pops and a long, low whirring sound. "Please stand by."

Seren sighed. "We need to get Shade to snap back from wherever she is. Lowkey, can you try to wake her up?"

He laid the girl down on the floor and she stared up into the ceiling lights, unblinking. "Shade? Wake up," he whispered in her ear. "Come back to us."

The girl gasped, and spoke in an odd rasp unlike her own lilting tone. "Insect. Insssect. Message for you. Kill you all, kill you all. Second time's the charm."

Lowkey recoiled from the girl. "What? What did you say?"

"Death comes for the mutants, disassembly for the 'bots. I'm coming."

Blinking hard, Shade sat upright. As she turned

toward Seren the light of consciousness returned to the girl's eyes. Whatever had possessed her was gone—or, at least, was once again suppressed. She looked back and forth between her surprised friends, frowning in confusion.

"She doesn't remember, any more than the ship computer remembers placing the implant in her head," Seren said. "Insect's smarter than I thought, and even more entrenched in the ship's systems."

Lowkey turned back to the arachnoid. "What's the damage, computer? What did Shade do to you?"

"The damage is repairable, but the data for the newly discovered planet has been corrupted. I believe the coordinates have been tampered with. I can no longer extrapolate useful information regarding its habitability."

"Do you still think we can find it? Maybe if we do another scan in its vicinity, fix those numbers…"

"Information missing. I can not reliably track this object again using any remaining data. The data which remains may be flawed. We must find a different planet to pursue. Our previous target is no longer worth the investment of fuel we would burn to pursue a potentially nonexistent destination. The numbers cannot be trusted."

"More wasted time," Lowkey said. "Insect is dragging this out, trying to prevent us from getting to the safety of a planet before he can find a way to kill us. If we didn't have the computer on our side, we'd be dead already."

"I know. And the computer is glitchy, too. Our resources are running thin."

"Request for further information," the arachnoid said. "Please define this 'glitch'. What happened on the day of Shade's revival, from your perspective?"

Lowkey glared. "Our 'perspective' is the only *true* perspective. You did the surgery you were supposed to do, but not until after you implanted some kind of data chip in Shade's head. Which you *weren't* supposed to do, by the way. In case that wasn't clear."

"I do not have any memory of this incident, but neither can I find any reason to believe you are lying. Please stand by."

The computer whirred as it ran internal checks on its memory database. Lowkey slid over to his bunk and dug around in his pack for a bottle, which he offered to Seren with a smile. "Breakfast?"

"Ugh. No. My throat still burns from yesterday's dinner."

The arachnoid spoke with a strange tone which sounded oddly embarrassed. "I have found an anomaly. It appears you were correct. I have been…tampered with."

"What was the chip for? Can you tell us now?"

"It was Insect's doing. He gave it to me, some time before the blast. The memory file of that interaction is corrupted. He is…in me, too. As he is in Shade."

Seren felt an adrenaline shot of ice-cold dread and she forced the panic back down. "If that's true, why aren't we dead yet?"

The little robot popped and buzzed, and its repair work slowed as it processed the enormity of its discovery. "He is…having fun. He is the hunter, you are the prey. And he will prolong this game as long as he can, as it is the last game he will ever play. He already killed all of the rest. You are the last."

"Oh my god. The explosion. It was him, wasn't it?"

"Yes. And…and Shade. He was the brain, but she was his hand. Although she does not appear to remember her actions."

Shade scowled at the arachnoid, and shook her head.

The little robot stood tall on its legs. "I stand by—

and urgently resubmit—my previous recommendation for your immediate consideration. Shade must be ejected from this room."

"We won't do it," Seren said. "You *know* we won't. She's important to us, get it? And she doesn't even remember doing any of that stuff. Can't you fix her? Remove the chip. You put it in her, you can take it out."

"Not without a carefully prepared room and a finely-tuned medical service robot. In my current form I could not perform the procedure without immense risk to the patient. The act of murder runs counter to my protocol, and the risk of unassisted brain surgery runs high enough that it would fall under the category of prohibited actions."

Shade rummaged through a plastic trunk and pulled out a ball of twine. She rolled it to Lowkey, who picked it up, frowning with confusion.

"Shade wants us to tie her up," Seren said.

"Fuck no! She's not a criminal. I won't do it."

"Lowkey, she's-"

"Shade would never hurt anyone. You should know her well enough to know that. She's innocent!"

"Okay, maybe she is. But Insect isn't, and he's inside her. She could shank you in your sleep, you know."

Shade smiled gently at Lowkey, and stroked his cheek with her fingertips. Nodding, she wrapped the twine loosely around her wrists, then held them out to him for help.

"Shit," Lowkey muttered. "I hate this. I really fucking hate this."

"This manner of restraint is insufficient," the computer said. "For your own safety, she must be ejected from-"

"Shut up," Seren hissed. "This is the most we're willing to do. So either get to work on finding us another planet, or get to work on finding a way to the medical labs so we can remove the imposter in Shade's brain which *you* put in there. Neither task requires talking to us right now, so choose one or the other and shut the fuck up."

The arachnoid buzzed, but said nothing more.

After Lowkey tied Shade's wrists, he helped her to a cot and sat her down. She gazed up at him with a lost, angelic expression, sad and accepting. He winced; his heart was breaking.

"We have work to do," Seren said. "And we're out of time. Now we know Insect is here, with us. He may be listening to our conversations. If he realizes he's been discovered, he might act quickly to end his game."

"Yeah. I know." Lowkey kissed Shade's forehead, and returned to sit near the arachnoid. "How can I help?"

"Our search needs to become a lot more aggressive. We'll take turns helping the computer sift through scans, resting in shifts. There's another planet out there just waiting for us but we need to find it fast. Insect will do everything he can to slow us down. It's time to stop dicking around. Let's make this happen."

"Nice pep talk," he grumbled. "Move over. I'll go first."

CHAPTER 16

WINDOWS TO SPY THROUGH

When Seren slept, her mind wandered.

It wasn't like dreaming, although the experience did bring with it the same hazy befuddlement which her dreams used to. But dreams stayed in the heads of their sleeping humans, while her rogue CPU drifted into other computerized components of the ship's complex AI as if drunkenly trying to find a way to help out, or perhaps just seeking a pleasant distraction. It worried her, but Seren needed the downtime, especially after redoubling her effort to find a habitable planet. She was too new to managing her complicated AI brain to prevent it from going on walkabout when she was resting.

As Lowkey took his third shift on the planet-seeking software—he was slower at it than she, but he still made some progress—the most fundamental level of her AI, a system which functioned like a subconscious mind, connected itself directly to the ship's cloud memory. It sniffed through directories, poked around the remaining functional eavesdropping speakers, and peeked through the cameras at the spider-infested hallways near the Gardens. It meandered toward the Core, then took a sharp left turn. There was something over there, between the Core and the Gardens. Something odd.

Seren tossed in her sleep, half-aware that she was laying on her cot in the safe room. "Nnn..." she could hear herself mumbling, trying to wake up. But her AI component had taken a special interest in its discovery. It found a functional camera in the dark area which had roused its interest, and turned it on.

A massive cavern had been excavated from the decks next to the Gardens, like a hole in an enormous Swiss cheese. It had been dug out and rebuilt with ladders, ramps, and Frankensteinian computers all cobbled together out of thousands of found components. Here was Insect's lair. It was his primary base of operations, where he spent every waking moment searching for new ways to undermine the ship's control and wreak havoc. Seven or eight service robots had been mounted on heavy robotic arms hanging from the ceiling, rotating on steel tracks to operate the input screens connected to the walls of computers. In the center of the room stood Insect himself, with his huge arms crossed, scowling at the robots. His extra legs hung at his sides draped in loose fabric. One appendage bled at his hip, from a deep gash which looked intentional; Insect's garb was neatly cut above the wound. Had he been trying to rid himself of the useless limbs which caused him so much pain?

Without warning, he whipped his head around to fix his eyes on the camera through which Seren spied. Her subconscious flinched, and she was torn from her dreaming state. She sat up in bed, gasping in shock. But her CPU's awareness lingered in the void a moment longer, peering into Insect's bloodshot eyes, seeking answers. Why was he so angry? And why was his rage directed at his mutant kindred, and at Seren?

She wrested her errant mind back from the cloud, forcing herself to full consciousness. How real was that encounter? It certainly seemed real enough. It was likely Insect had been able to perceive her presence to some extent, understanding his hiding place had been found. But had he looked back, seen into the safe room?

"Computer, do you know anything about what just happened? Did you see that?"

"You must improve your ability to control your own AI, Seren. Neglecting to do so is dangerous and foolhardy. I do not think Insect was able to look back at you. But you can not keep doing this."

"I don't know how to stop! I'm new at being an AI. No one ever taught me anything. How do I keep my shit together when I'm on downtime?"

"Take over for Lowkey and start your shift. I will teach you. But you have learned something important about our enemy, haven't you?"

"Maybe. Insect has computers. Tons of them. Walls full of them. He's gaining on us fast, and he will find us soon. But I still don't know why."

Lowkey rose from his seat on the floor and stretched his arms, raising his shirt enough for Seren to see his green stomach. Tiny dark-green hairs grew below his navel. He caught her looking, but he was too tired to make fun.

"Your turn. I gotta sleep," he mumbled. "I didn't find shit. Good luck."

~

Halfway through Seren's shift, she took a break from searching—and from the computer's dreary lecture on How To Be A Better Robot—to check on Shade. The twine on the girl's wrists had rubbed the skin until it was white and raw, but she still wore a smile on her face. Once, two nights ago, she had tried to chew through the restraint. But it hadn't really been her doing that. It was Insect, manipulating her through her implant, trying to free his pet. Seren had to put a piece of cloth in the girl's mouth to prevent her from chewing on her own flesh as she tried to remove the twine. Insect's control over her was violent but imprecise, and he did not care about her well-being. To him, she was just another service robot.

But Shade was herself today. She sat up and licked her lips. Hungry. Seren spoon-fed her heaping bites of chocolate pudding.

"Shade, I have to ask you a difficult question. It's one which Insect won't want you to answer, but I need you to try. Okay?"

She nodded.

"Insect is accessing your brain through the chip he made the computer install in your head, but I was wondering if you can look back at him. Can you get anything from his transmissions which might help us protect ourselves from him? And this is the most important question of all: why is he hunting us?"

Shade turned a paler shade of aqua. Each question made her wince. She was afraid to answer, afraid of drawing Insect's attention back to her. But she understood the importance of what Seren was asking. And there was only one way to respond. She would have to speak aloud.

She opened her mouth, and tried a sound. "Aaah."

Seren smiled, encouraging.

"Insect…won't let me t…" She closed her eyes and raised her bound hands, rubbing them together. "Talk. Since the implant."

"Yeah, I guessed it was something like that. Is it difficult?"

"Not exactly. But it…hurts."

"He's hurting you because all he knows is pain. I'm so sorry, Shade."

"The chip. Causes pain. To talk. But you must know why. I need to tell you."

Seren leaned forward. This question, above all others, felt the most important to her. "Please, if you can. I'm so sorry it hurts you, but please try."

"The connection is Dr. Roberts."

As soon as the girl spoke his name she keeled forward, screaming in agony. Lowkey leapt from his cot, reaching for the laser gun before Seren could stop him. He aimed at Shade with his shaking finger hovering over the trigger.

Seren leaped between him and Shade, holding her hands up. "Lowkey! Stop, it's okay! She's still tied up!"

Aghast, he threw the gun into the corner and fell to his knees, sobbing. "I was still half-asleep…didn't know…"

Shade stopped screaming, and the light went from her eyes. She had checked out again.

Seren knelt by Lowkey, and after a moment of hesitation she wrapped him in her arms. "You didn't know. Shade isn't always Shade, anymore. I'm so sorry. It's not your fault. Anyway, you didn't actually shoot her."

"But I aimed a gun at her, Seren. I…"

"Not your fault. Blame Insect. Blame me, even. I made her talk."

"She spoke?"

"There is a connection between Insect and the scientist who created me. I think Insect's rage is personal, against me and your mutant family. He blasted the ship but he missed a few people, and they were some of the ones he wanted most to kill. Shade needed me to know, and she put herself through terrible pain to tell me."

"Ugh, I'm a complete piece of shit."

"She can't be trusted. You weren't wrong. It's okay."

"Is she really all right? That screaming…"

"I don't think she's any worse off than she was before. The chip causes artificial pain. It tells the brain that horrible pain is occurring, but there's no real damage to the body. It functions in a similar way to my own protocol, which tells me when I should be feeling emotion and physical sensation."

The arachnoid clicked. "Seren, I believe I may have discovered data connecting Insect to Dr. Roberts. I have video playback of certain incidents which pertain to your questions. You should watch them, but you may find them disturbing."

"That's…good. I understand. Just give me a minute." Seren turned to Lowkey. "Uh…you have any more of the pink stuff? Or even the blue stuff?"

"Fresh out. Only have a few bottles of brown."

"Bring it on."

The arachnoid robot raised its view screen and started playback.

~

Something was blocking the camera. Gray fabric, being pulled across the lens. It moved aside and came into focus for a moment: a man's shirt, dotted with tiny blue flowers. A figure lay on a table, covered in a crisp white sheet: a woman, screaming in pain. Giving birth.

A service robot waited between her legs. Soft green legs, hairless, vulnerable. But the woman's knees were blushed with a whisper of pink.

The baby arrived, taken into the robot's extended arm. It screamed and writhed, then quickly calmed, observing its surroundings with wide open eyes. It had already adapted to its environment, graduating from terror and shock to eager exploration in mere seconds.

"Green! Damn it to hell!" A man, with his back to the camera, shouted into the woman's face. "I need pink…or brown…anything that comes even *remotely* close to a real skin tone!"

The woman sobbed, reaching for her baby.

A voice from somewhere off screen asked, "Shall we incinerate the child?"

"Let her keep it. We will try again with a different female. Perhaps we will be able to use this one for organs, some time in the future…but perhaps not. It appears to have inherited the fast-aging gene, which makes it essentially useless. Look at this, the navel is already healed."

The screen faded to black, and opened on a new scene. It was another birth. A different mother, in the same room, on the same table. She had pale skin, not pink or brown but lavender. The scientist knelt to peer between her legs, and Seren gasped when she recognized his face from her sharpest, realest memories.

"Oh god. It's him. Dr. Roberts. He was…*breeding* mutants."

Lowkey's face wrenched with disgust. "That first baby, it was me, wasn't it? I don't remember my mother. But the skin…"

The scientist shouted at the woman as she bore down. "Give me a color, honey! A real one. None of this green and blue bullshit."

But the baby came out like a brilliant sapphire, the most gorgeous blue—and two extra limbs, boneless and frail, hung from its hips.

"Insect," Lowkey whispered.

The scientist on the screen railed against the woman. She sobbed, reaching for her baby, but the man was outraged and demanded the robot incinerate the child.

"No more mouths to feed!" he shouted. "We must try again until we have something we can use. I already have half a dozen in this color. We're out of room to store mistakes!"

The infant blinked and stopped crying, just as the green baby had. Its arms were twice the size as a human child's, and already shaped by tiny muscles.

Seren cleared her throat. "Computer? Insect escaped incineration, didn't he?"

"Correct. And, some time later, he learned exactly how he had come to be."

"But how is any of this *my* fault? I'm just as much a victim of Dr. Roberts as he is. I never asked to be born either."

The scientist on the screen ordered the woman to be removed from the room, and the monitor faded to a new scene.

A young child, just one or two years old, lay on a table. Her skin was soft and smooth and humanoid tan, with no trace of any cooler tones. She had a redundant arm growing from her side, and seven fingers on her left hand. Aside from those differences, she could have been a human child.

From her left leg a swath of skin was missing, as was her right foot.

"No. No, no, no…" Seren shook her head. "No. I refuse to believe-"

Lowkey's face wrenched with nausea and horror. When he directed his shocked expression toward Seren she burst into tears. He hissed with low revulsion when he spoke. "Dr. Roberts was harvesting. He discovered the mutant babies, took them from their mothers, kept them secret, and bred them as they quickly matured. So he could reap pieces of their living bodies to create things like *you*."

"Not my fault. I didn't know. I-"

"No fucking wonder. No fucking wonder why Insect hates you, hates all of us. Some of us were born naturally, the result of some kind of anomaly in space during gestation. But the rest of the mutant population was created by your father, to provide his project…to provide *you*…with spare parts."

"Don't call him my father!" Seren heard herself scream. Her voice rang loud in her ears as rage clenched her hands into fists. "I hate him! I hate him as much as any of you *ever* could!"

But Lowkey turned his head, unable to look at her. And Seren ran out of the safe house, down the corridors, fleeing once again for the comfort of solitude.

CHAPTER 17

PESTILENCE

Seren ran down the corridors, screaming her enemy's name. She knew where his lair was, and what he was trying to do. So why had she let him continue his hunt for so long?

"Insect!" She screamed his name, sending it out to echo along the walls and halls of the *Resolution*. "Come at me! This is over. Show yourself, you coward!"

It would take time to reach the Core, unless she could draw him out. She ran faster than she had ever been able to when she thought she was human. When her legs started to complain, she cut the message off. Faster and faster toward his lair, to the growing infestation at the center of the ship.

"I know you can hear me. I know you're always listening. Stop hiding, and do what you have been working toward all this time. Come and kill me, if you can!"

Even in her rage, Seren noted the spread of decay which had permeated the ship. The walls were alternating hot and cold to the touch, as the environmental temperature regulation systems had started to fail. Many panels were streaked with black mold and fungus growing from a plethora of leaks sprung from unmaintained plumbing. The floors were indented with ruts where service robots had rolled over and over on their metal wheels, in their relentless search for Seren and her friends.

Insect did not answer her challenge.

She neared the Gardens. A set of large double doors had been torn from its hinges, providing an open view of Pine Forest #2. But it was no longer a forest. The trees had been blasted to splinters. The metal panels on the far walls which had once been hidden by the trunks of old firs were now laid bare, streaked with mud and pitted by laser fire. The only remaining creatures which still moved were spiders—millions of them, spinning cotton-candy webs among the shattered trees in thick blankets. Hovering near the sun-lights at the ceiling was their prey, countless gnats swarming in black tornadoes. If Seren didn't find a habitable planet for the mutants, this terrarium of pests would be the successors of the final legacy of life in the galaxy.

Prying her eyes from the ruin of the forest, Seren called again. "Insect! Confront me, *now!* I'm tired of this game. At least talk to me!"

"You've no right to speak to me." The voice came from an eavesdropper speaker set into the corridor wall.

"I understand now why you're angry. But listen, it wasn't my fault. I didn't ask-"

"You inherited fault. Your patchwork body carries the burden of your origin, and I will lift that burden from your stolen shoulders in the moments before I destroy the remains of this drifting coffin."

"If I give myself to you, will you spare my friends?"

"If you give yourself to me, they will die anyway. They will never find a new planet without your help. I know the connection you have with that *bitch* AI. They don't have it."

Seren moved near the eavesdropper to speak in a more intimate voice. "You can be with us, Insect. We would welcome you. We can all work together to find a way off this ship, and then you won't have to be alone any more."

After a pause, Insect responded in a humble tone.

"Tell me more. I'm listening."

"With your help, we'd find a new planet even faster. We're looking for a place which can support life. Real soil, plants, and breathable air. You'd have a new family, with me and Lowkey and Shade. And we could all look out for each other."

"Sounds so nice…"

Something moved into the corridor behind her. It wasn't a robot. Its feet were soft and damp, sticking to the floor. She turned and found Shade, but it wasn't Shade. Her eyes were empty, and in her hand she held a sharp triangular shard of metal. The girl's feet were lacerated, oozing blood onto the floor panels. She had run after Seren, ignoring the pain in her feet and lungs at Insect's command. The look in her red, wide eyes showed an intense desire for murder.

Insect laughed, a sound so loud and abrasive it sent crackles through the wall speaker before it blew out and went dead.

"Shade," Seren whispered. "It's me. Please wake up. You can't harm me, not really. I'm a robot, or a cyborg… whatever. Insect is using you to hurt me, because I…" She stopped, surprised. But her impulse was true, and she wanted to speak it. "I love you, Shade. And I love Lowkey. Can you understand? It's not…it goes against my protocol to have this emotional response. But it's true anyway. Don't believe Insect. I'm your friend, no matter what. Do you hear me?"

The girl closed her eyes, and her grip on the metal shard tightened. It cut into her palm, sending a gush of blood spilling to the floor in a steady stream which pooled with the trickle from her feet.

Insect was slicing the girl apart.

Shade raised the shard to her own neck, but Seren could see she was fighting the movement. The girl's eyes rolled behind her closed lids, and her mouth stretched into a grimace. Seren hesitated to interfere. She might distract the girl from her fight, or make her struggle even harder. And more than that, she sensed it was important for Shade to learn how to sever her connection with Insect on her own, without outside help.

The shard pressed into the skin of the girl's neck as the muscles in her arm bulged. Her forearm fought to move the metal closer as her biceps tried to throw it away.

"You can do it," Seren whispered. "Find him, find his hiding place inside you and expel him."

A service robot rolled around the corner and paused, taking in the scene. It raised a gun but did not fire. Perhaps Insect had sent it as insurance against their survival.

As the metal began to pierce a hole her neck, Shade's eyes flew open. She brought her other hand up to push the shard away, her fingers slipping in her own dripping blood. It sliced at her hands as she pried, cutting away more flesh, but she persisted until she held the shard in front of her body at arm's length.

It was enough. Seren grabbed the metal and pried it away from the girl's fingers, casting it aside. Shade fell into her arms, exhausted and weeping.

The service robot beeped, but still it held its fire. Seren grabbed Shade's wrist and pulled her down the hall toward the Gardens, and the robot did not follow.

~

They tumbled from the eleva-tree into Pine Forest #5, soaked in blood. This forest looked much like the other Seren had seen, with trees blasted and most of the animals gone. They staggered through the scorched pine needles, past splintered trunks jutting up from the shallow soil like listing skyscrapers. Seren did not expect to find much left of the Treehouse.

But some of it yet remained. It had been cut from its perch, but had fallen in such a way as to form a slanted pyramid under which they crawled, taking comfort in the darkness there. The blankets were unsoiled, and Seren used strips of the fabric to bind Shade's cuts. A bottle of water also remained, just enough to rinse their wounds and wet their mouths.

"I think that service robot went to get help," Seren whispered. "We need to stay hidden."

Shade nodded, and sipped water. "I…agree."

"You're speaking again?"

"It hurts, but not like before. The implant is still in my brain. But his influence is weakened. Thank you, Seren."

"Me? Why?"

"For not helping me. I learned how to quiet his voice in my head. He's in a cage now, behind a locked door. I can still hear him yelling, but he has no control over me. At least, not at the moment."

"That's good, but you almost died."

"Still, you made the right choice. See? I can talk now. There's this pounding feeling, a piercing pain in my skull, flashes of light…"

"Sounds like a migraine."

"Migraine? I don't know what that means. But still, the pain is bearable. And it's nice to talk to you, Seren. Seren, Seren, Seren."

Seren raised her eyebrows. "Hmm?"

"It feels nice to say your name. Because I love you too, Seren. You are my sister."

Warmth bloomed in Seren's chest. It was a feeling she should not have been able to experience, if she was a machine. But Lowkey was right. Her existence was complex. She was no service robot. And if it was in her power to do so, she would leave her protocol behind.

"I'm faint…" Shade leaned back, holding her lacerated hands to her chest.

"You've lost a lot of blood, but not enough to put you in danger. You should sleep for a little while. I'll keep watch."

"Thank you."

As Shade fell asleep, Seren admired at the girl's smooth aqua skin, enjoying a rush of gentle affection which, at last, she no longer felt the need to deny.

"Found you." Lowkey peeked under the leaning wooden wall.

"Get in here before the robots see you," Seren whispered.

"You shouldn't have run away."

"I thought you hated me. The way you were looking at me…"

"I'm sorry. The video really bothered me. I never knew about all of that."

"Neither did I. Please, you have to believe me."

"I do. What's with her?" Lowkey nodded at Shade. "She ran out right after you did."

"Insect guided her to me, tried to make her kill me. She fought him, and won. Her wounds are pretty bad but I think she'll be okay. And she's talking now."

"What? Seriously?"

Seren nodded. "She found a way to weaken Insect's link to her implant."

"Um…" Lowkey winced. "I hate to say this, but we still can't trust her. He could be listening."

"You're right, he could be. But our choice is simple. We can either keep her with us and accept the risk, or leave her behind."

Lowkey nodded. "Right. I'm not leaving her."

"I know. Neither am I. She's my sister. And she's… whatever she is to you."

"What does that mean?"

Seren shrugged, and wondered if she was blushing. She had no idea if it was something she had been designed to do. "You love her."

"Of course I do. And I think you do, too."

"Yes, but…it's different. Right?"

"How?"

"You are…you know. Together."

Lowkey's eyebrows shot up. "We aren't lovers, if that's what you mean."

"Well, no, but only because everything is so fucked up. I mean, if we were safe, and everything was normal…"

He grinned. "She's your sister, and she's my sister, but that doesn't mean you and I are siblings."

"She's only a sister? But you two are so…you know, close. Physically."

Lowkey shrugged. "Not in the way you mean. She needs my protection. Not like you. You're powerful, amazing…"

"Pink."

"I can look past that." He leaned forward and brushed his lips against her cheek.

Seren gasped. Had anyone ever touched her with such tenderness before? Her programmed false memories of parental affection and previous lovers disappeared in that moment, and she was struck with the knowledge that this was the first time she had ever been caressed by another person. "More," she whispered, brushing her lips against his cheek. "Again. *Please.*"

He leaned into her, took her in his arms, and held her. Her AI brain screamed, "*More, more…*" but she accepted what he was only willing to offer in that moment—genuine affection in a firm embrace. If there was also passion, he hid it in favor of providing her with loving care and soft kindness which her soul drank in like water from an oasis.

CHAPTER 18

THE ORIGINS OF THE END

Seren spent half an hour brushing cobwebs off of the Treehouse rafters and windows. They stuck to her fingers, wrapping around her gloves until she rolled the mess off in little fuzzy white balls. The spiders were the only living creatures on the ship which were still thriving. They had created a new civilization of their own amid the ruins of the *Resolution*, weaving complex structures which connected the splinters and remnants of the remains of humanity's last hope into a vast gossamer network. They first overpopulated the pine forests, then migrated in swarms to the corridors, the mess halls, the crew's private quarters. Only the Core, under the continued maintenance of its special upper-class robots, was free of their presence.

She combined several clumps of web into one huge compacted snowball and lobbed it out through the shattered porthole window. The Treehouse rested at an awkward angle but the furniture and most of the other items inside were unbroken, due to its soft landing on the forest's thick bed of pine needles. The only access to the inside left by the structure's tilt was a crack in the broken siding. But eventually the service robots would check this place again as they made their rounds, and if they looked carefully they would notice the gap. Seren had no idea what to do about that.

When Shade awoke, she was despondent. She sat up, but did not move from her pile of blankets. She stared down at the floor in an absent manner which worried Seren. Was the girl checking out again? But Insect was gone from her consciousness—or, at least, no longer in charge of his vessel.

Lowkey stirred and awoke, reaching for a bottle and finding none. "Well now we're really in trouble," he muttered. "You won't like me when I'm sober."

The sound of his voice roused Shade from her stupor. She gazed up at him and held out her arms for a hug.

He dutifully complied, and sat next to her. "So, I hear you're talking now."

"A little. It's still uncomfortable, but I think that's just conditioning. I'm used to the pain being overwhelming. Now it's just a dull ache, nothing I can't handle."

"You don't have to say anything if you don't want to. You can keep quiet."

"No. I have something important to say. I can't be quiet any longer."

Seren sat across from the pair. "What is it?"

"I am…" Shade hid her face behind her bandaged hands. Her body heaved with a silent sob. "Responsible. For everything."

"Look, Shade, there's just no way you're-"

"*All* of it! Insect used me, but it was my hand which set the bomb. I laid the line, pulled the trigger…I remember it all. The chip the computer implanted wasn't the beginning. I've been working for him for a long time. He fed me instructions and punished me when I disobeyed. But I should have been stronger! I didn't know how bad it would be, how powerful the bomb was or that it was planted next to one of the fuel tanks. I had no idea it would release toxic chemicals throughout the ship. I thought maybe it would just take out a little bit of engineering, you know? The *bad* part. I kind of knew how rotten Dr. Roberts was, I'd heard rumors. And I thought if he died the whole ship might be better off.

I never hated the humans. Not like Insect did. Most of them were stupid but harmless, really."

Shade paused, panting, rubbing her temples with her fingertips. All four of her eyes squeezed shut as every word drained her energy, sent pulses of aching pain through her head.

"We don't blame you, Shade." Lowkey draped his arm around her shoulders, but she pushed it off.

"No. Let me talk before you decide."

~

The aqua-tinted baby was yet another disappointment in a long line of failures. She was rejected, sent back to her mother after a dossier of her working parts had been created: strong heart, two redundant eyes in addition to two natural ones, three working lungs, possibly above-average intellect. But of course she carried the pervasive fast-aging gene, an unfortunately common flaw. Even the girl's mother was largely disinterested in her. Giving birth had not been the woman's choice, and she was unable to emotionally separate the trauma of her insemination from the child itself. Service robots tended to the infant's basic needs, but it was not until she was old enough to make friends, at about a year and a half, that she experienced any physical touch or personal connection with other people.

Her mother disappeared soon after giving birth, and the girl never discovered her true fate. Maybe the woman found a way to evade Dr. Roberts, escaped his mutant lockup—or perhaps she was cut up and used for spare parts.

When the girl met Lowkey, she was instantly enthralled. He was a little older than she, and far more physically powerful. He also wielded an unaffected charisma which she yearned to emulate. Even as a child he protected her and taught her how to survive, all while calling her silly names like "sprout" and acting like he didn't care. And she didn't mind it at all, because even as a child she understood that his behavior was his way of protecting himself from pain. He had lost many friends over his short years on the ship, and he had learned not to become attached.

By the time she was four years old she could run fast enough to accompany him on food raids. They stole from commissaries, mess halls, food manufactories. Once they made off with a huge wheel of fancy cheese from a posh Core restaurant.

As the years passed, Lowkey taught her everything he knew about accessing information from the ship computer. She stole classes in math, science, human history, and art. By the time she was seven years old she had surpassed him in every school of knowledge, developed a razor-sharp wit, and had even taken on some of his signature cynicism and generally rebellious nature. More than once, her intelligence prevailed when Lowkey's strength did not. As his respect for the girl grew, he started calling her by the name she had chosen for herself: Shade. And despite the boy's attempt at keeping his heart callous, their bond grew unbreakable.

During one of their forays into the upper-class human quarters for supplies, they became separated. They were near the Core that day, trying to find some kind of soft nutrition for a rejected newborn. Lowkey was also hoping for some real medicine, which only the upper-class humans had access to. After he crawled ahead through the ducting to check for guards, Shade was distracted by something sparkly. The most beautiful lights she had ever seen glimmered brighter than the stars through a heating vent which opened onto one of the grand courtyards. She crept close to peek between the slats.

The humans had erected an enormous tree, thirty feet tall, right in the center of the courtyard. She could see right away it wasn't real but made of plastic, and studded with a thousand—no, *ten* thousand twinkling lights. The sparkles were reflected in countless shiny baubles hanging from the branches, and perched at the top of the tree was a human-shaped figurine with spread-open bird wings.

The entire display was glorious nonsense. A human with extra limbs could only be a kind of mutant, yet the humans hated and feared mutants. She could not believe they would revere one, even if it had wings.

Had they lost their minds? She had to see more.

She picked at the vent's screws with her fingertips until they were loose, and she pushed it free of its frame. The opening was barely wide enough even for her tiny body, but she inched her way through like a caterpillar and eventually tumbled to the lush carpet. She dashed to hide behind a luxurious sofa just in time to watch a flashy couple walk by, adorned in bright red and green clothing complete with felt hats and false pointed ears. Another man stumbled past wearing deer antlers on his head and a round red nose, slurping whiskey from a rainbow-colored glass. Their garments were silly but happy, and everything about the celebration appeared to be in appreciation of mutants. Many of the humans were grinning and laughing, but they did not seem to have gone mad. They were cheerful and relaxed.

One of the humans dug around under the tree and pulled out a box wrapped in gorgeous silver paper topped with a green bow. They tore the wrapping to shreds, but inside they discovered something inside which was even better. Something which made their face beam with joy.

So much laughter, so much pleasure. But *why?* She had to get closer.

Shade crawled on her belly to the next sofa set, and hid behind a rack of media tablets. The closest shining box was only twenty feet away. It had gold paper with a red bow. If she ran fast enough…

A strong hand grasped the nape of her neck, and another squeezed her arm. She was pulled backward, away from the celebration, and thrown into a dim maintenance closet.

"Almost lost you there," a voice said in the darkness. "I've been watching you for too long to let them catch you now."

"Who are you? Let me go!"

"I'm your new boss. You should feel very fortunate. Out of all the little mutie kids, you're my favorite. And look…I'm just like you." The speaker moved into a narrow ray of light near the door and bared his arm from underneath a draping cloak. His skin was dark blue.

"You're a mutant too! Why are you kidnapping me?"

"I'll let you go in a minute. First, open your mouth."

"No. Why should I?"

The man jammed his hand between her teeth, wrenching her jaw open. On his thumb he wore a steel claw which he used to pierce the top of her mouth. Into the deep gash he pressed a tiny data chip, tucking it under her flesh, and held it there until the wound knit itself shut with mutant speed.

The next moment, he was gone. Shade was alone in the closet, poking at the scar with her tongue. It didn't hurt, and she didn't feel any different. What had that been all about?

Three weeks passed, and she almost forgot about the strange encounter. But she started to have bad dreams. In them, a four-legged man talked to her about the futility of life, the evil of humans, the joy of destruction. Specific details of the dreams grew hazy after she awoke each morning, but the sense of dread she felt during those nightly lectures carried into the days, and she became withdrawn in her exhaustion.

On the days when she was particularly tired, she experienced odd urges she could neither ignore nor deny. The gathering of certain items—such as empty casings, jars of chemicals, maps of the engineering decks— happened while she was in a daze, drifting through the heating ducts, answering some silent call. She could remember her yearning to collect the items and the hard work she did to obtain them, but after leaving each stupor her conscious thoughts became muddled and dissociated. Far stronger than her memory of her labor was the satisfaction she felt whenever she completed a task. The sensation of achievement was more addictive than sugary soda, and it came in a great rush of gratification every time a quota was filled.

And then the final day came. Her ultimate goal was close. She felt it, the looming conclusion. The end. Her memories from that day were stronger; her consciousness cut through the haze and started to retain more clarity after she started fighting against the urges, as her true self began to piece together what her work might be. Whatever she was assembling, it was no good thing. It would cause death.

It happened on her eighth birthday. She had wanted to celebrate it as any sixteen-year-old human girl might—good food, time to rest, maybe an adventure with friends. But the urge to collect invaded her mind early that day. She should find something flammable, something combustible, something to purge evil and cast a bright glowing light which could defeat the spreading darkness.

What spreading darkness?

An hour after rising from bed she found herself in a crawlspace near the engineering decks, running a long line which weaved through a maze of connected shafts. The line connected a device and a button. She remembered making the device. That job was done two weeks ago, and she had been proud.

Why?

The wire which connected the button to the device was a mile long. The device was was attached to a box, and inside the box was a bomb. The bomb was tiny, the size of an apple, but its size didn't matter. The explosion it was capable of it would be the brightest thing ever, bright as a supernova. And it would purge the universe of the greatest evil, to stop an infection before it spread. It would destroy the last humans.

How did she know that?

Shade's consciousness poked through her stupor. Kill the humans? *All* of them? But they built this ship. They were the source of her food, of her air. They were arrogant and frightened and flawed, and most of them didn't even know people like her existed. But they were also the providers and the progenitors. She didn't want them to die.

She shook her head. "No! I won't do it. Get out of my head!"

A skewer of pain stabbed her palate and spread into her teeth. From there the agony grew, searing her eyes, piercing the center of her brain. She collapsed inside the ventilation shaft, writhing on the dusty metal sheeting until she gave in and reached for the button. The moment her finger brushed it, the pain ceased.

"No," she sobbed. "Don't make me. *Please.*"

She thrashed in the shaft, fighting her urges, but she could not drop the trigger. It was clasped tight in her disobedient hand. When she went limp with pain and collapsed, her head fell near a vent.

Through the slats she saw a man talking to another man. They were too far away for their conversation to be audible, but both seemed upset. An exhausted lab technician, dressed all in white, was arguing with a man in a dirty pea-green smock who Shade recognized as Dr. Roberts, the enemy of mutants. He was the reason for her birth, but also for her misery. He had taken her away from her mother.

Surely it was worth a few civilian losses to ensure his life ended. He was evil. Maybe the other humans weren't, but he was. Beyond any doubt.

Her finger twitched over the button. Were these her own thoughts, or did they belong to the one who had inserted himself into her?

Her gaze shifted to the other man. He was peach-colored, as a good number of the humans were, but his cheeks were blushed with rage. Such delicate tones the humans wore, pink and tan and brown, so pretty and warm. She had no wish to harm the man, especially as he seemed to be arguing with Dr. Roberts. He didn't deserve to die, did he?

But whatever the disagreement was about, the technician lost his side. He nodded, scowling at the floor, as Dr. Roberts spun on his heel and strode from the room with a smug look on his face. The man turned to a computer and brought up a projected hologram of a young mutant with soft green skin: Lowkey. The man wiped his eyes, groaning, and raised his hand to the image. After a final moment of hesitation, he touched a box next to the word "euthanize."

"No…" Shade whispered in the dark. "No! No, no, *no!*"

Shouting with rage, she pressed the button.

In the second before the powerful blast blew her back through the ventilation duct, she saw the man's body torn in half. The look of dismayed shock on his soft face burned in her memory.

~

Shade stopped speaking.

Tears, glinting in the light of the emergency lantern, trickled down her cheeks. "I can't say any more. It's all dark after that, for a long time."

Lowkey brushed Shade's hair back from her eyes. "That's when I found you. You survived the blast, although I don't know how. Your skin was abraded and burned, and you were unconscious, so I carried you back to our quarters and tended to you for weeks. When you took a turn for the worse I put you into a stasis chamber. I was never able to wake you up. If you weren't a mutant, you'd have died."

"You should have let me die."

"Don't say that."

"It doesn't matter. We're all going to die anyway. We can't avoid Insect forever, and the chances of us finding a new planet are extremely remote. We're hanging on to nothing."

"No," Seren said. "Please, don't give up. We can keep trying…"

"Easy for you to say." Lowkey scowled at her. "You're still not in any real danger, are you? I mean, Insect could blow you up, I guess. But you're not scared, and you don't even have to feel pain if you're not in the mood for it. If we run out of food, or air, or water, you'll be fine. What's at stake for you, anyway?"

"My friends."

"Says your AI brain, programmed to act human. Look, I *know* you have feelings. But the fact that you can turn them off-"

"Makes no difference. I won't let you quit. You saved me, not long ago. At the oxy-lobby. Why did you bother? My life was essentially over. The old Seren died that day. You pulled my body back in, but I'll never be the same. Why?"

Lowkey shrugged, and muttered, "It wasn't right. Suicide isn't the answer, no matter what."

"Right. And giving up is suicide, and I won't let you do that. Let's all get some rest, okay? Especially you, Shade."

The girl winced. "I don't deserve your care. I am a murderer."

Seren took her shoulders in her hands and forced herself into the girl's line of sight. "No. Insect is responsible for everything. I know what it's like to not be in control of your own life. Never, *ever* doubt his culpability. You are innocent, do you hear me?"

Shade nodded, but stared down at her bandages, refusing to look at Seren's face.

"One more thing," Seren said. "I want to thank you for being honest. I know it was hard, but now we know everything there is to know, and it's a step in the right direction."

"Not everything," Shade mumbled.

"What?"

"Not everything." Fresh tears rolled down her cheeks. "I have one more thing to say. He's in you too, Seren. You didn't figure that out yet? You're an AI. You communicate directly with the computer. Insect is a virus, and he's in you too."

Seren sat back, stunned. She had never considered the likelihood that Insect had access to her CPU through the cloud…but of course he would have.

"Have I, uh, behaved strangely?"

"Not in the way I have. But he's in your head, and he's a ticking time bomb. The only one of us truly free of his direct influence is Lowkey."

He grunted. "That's me, pure and innocent. But hey, Seren, I promise if you go batshit and try to kill us I'll put a laser hole in your head. I won't let you suffer."

"This isn't the time for jokes."

Lowkey stared through her with bloodshot eyes. "Maybe I wasn't joking."

CHAPTER 19

GEAR UP, GET DOWN

Seren was adrift in boundless space.

Incalculable celestial bodies, too numerous for even her exceptional CPU to count, hung suspended in the void. Her physical being was plodding, linear, and clumsy. Its movement through the emptiness was at a standstill, its existence inconsequential. She was nothing but a speck of overcomplicated dust: a life-preserving generation ship filled with corpses, a failure, impossibly far from its origin. She was the *G.S.S. Resolution*, and she was also nothing at all.

Drifting in the quiet. Alone…then, abruptly, not alone.

Her scanners detected another body, not far away and much like her own. It was made of the same components as she: steel and glass, fuel and electricity, overgrown plants and rotten flesh. The chances of that were not just improbable, they were practically impossible, given the distance she had traveled and the vastness of space. But there it was, a shape not dissimilar to her own shape, aside from the fact that it was whole.

Its engineering decks were intact.

Seren directed her communications system to hail it, before remembering she was dreaming.

And, of course, *she* was not the ship.

She opened her eyes. "Computer! Did you see that?"

"See what, Cadet Seren?"

"There's another ship! I think it's a sister ship to the *Resolution*, one of the originals from Earth! It's out there and it's close, about nineteen thousand miles off the port side."

"There's nothing on my radar…stand by." The arachnoid clicked and popped. "I am…astonished, Seren. How did you make this discovery?"

"I'm sorry. I guess I was hitchhiking again."

The arachnoid buzzed with irritation.

"That's beside the point. Just *look*."

"Standard G.S.S. class American generation starship. Condition unknown. Population unknown. No automated response to hails."

"Can we get to it?"

"Cadet Seren, we have enough thruster fuel for approximately two and a half more directional adjustments. It should be assumed one adjustment will be used to initiate movement toward a final planet investigation, and one more will be necessary for course correction in the inevitable event of a slight error in navigational calculations. It is my fond hope we will have enough fumes leftover to slow our approach before we collide with said planet. We do not have the resources to explore derelict crafts."

"But it's a ship. From *Earth*. We have to go take a look. And what if they have more thruster fuel?"

"Let's do it!" Lowkey said.

Shade sat up from her nest of blankets. "Yes, please, Seren. Make the computer take us there."

"I can't make the computer do anything."

"That is correct," the arachnoid replied. "However, I concur with the consensus. The chances of our discovery of a fully habitable planet are minuscule, while the chances of finding usable resources on the derelict are high. You may yet fend off death for a short time longer if we succeed at this attempt."

Lowkey's face fell. "You don't have to say it like that. I just wanted to go on a little adventure."

"You will stay here, as will Shade. Seren will travel to the other ship, and I will accompany her."

"No way! We're going too!"

"It is far too dangerous. Seren's robotic augments will help protect her from the most probable hazards. You two are vulnerable, and will stay here. If you wish, you may monitor our progress on a comm."

Shade comforted Lowkey as he scowled. "Computer is right. We should stay."

"Seren, you must outfit yourself with a Regency suit. While you do not need the oxygen supply, we should assume the air temperature will be low and the atmosphere will be nonexistent, which will reduce your functionality. The suit will protect the parts of you which are flesh, and insulate the parts which are mechanical."

"How will I get to the derelict?"

"I have a shuttle ready, but it is short-range. First we must move to within two miles of the derelict. I will adjust our trajectory now. You do not need to take shelter, as the thrusters will only fire at half power. Of greater concern is the approach of numerous service robots. They are making their rounds, and they are well armed. You will not reach the shuttle without encountering them unless you crawl through the ventilation system."

"Damn it!" Seren sat in the corner with her head in her hands. "This has to stop. We can't go on like this. Insect won't confront me directly, and we're running out of time. He's going to find us and kill us in a matter of days, if not hours."

Lowkey nodded. "There's only one option left, and it's a risk."

"What do you mean?"

"I have that little laser pistol from the captain's desk, but it's just not enough. We never did find the armory Shade showed us on her tablet. I tried to find a direct route, but its exact position relative to the corridors isn't marked on the maps, probably for security reasons. We need to find and access it if we're going to have any real shot at survival. It would mean a lot more dodging from service robots and ducking through ventilation shafts, but if you could get there we would have a fighting chance. It won't just have guns, either. You should be able to find vacuum-proof armor, tools…"

"Right. Computer, can you lead me to the armory?"

"Cadets do not have clearance, even to the knowledge of the existence of the armory."

"Okay, well. Can you?"

"Yes."

Lowkey grinned. "Nice. Hey, bring me back a few grenades, okay? And more matches, if there are any."

"When I leave the forest, any remaining eavesdroppers will hear me. The service robots will probably figure out pretty quickly where you're hiding. You'll be in danger."

"Yeah. If they come, we'll fight. What else do we have left at this point? A broken Treehouse, one tiny gun, a pile of blankets, rations for a day or two…"

"And no booze."

"Not a single bottle. Might as well be dead."

Seren looked up at Shade. "And her? Are you going to ask her to fight?"

Shade scowled. "I can speak now, you don't have to talk about me like I'm not here. I think…we should stay here and hide, not fight. We're good at hiding."

The arachnoid folded its display monitor into its torso compartment. "Shade is correct. Seren will find the armory, then return to the Gardens. If you are discovered before she returns, she will proceed directly to the shuttle instead. The mutants will both stay hidden for as long as possible. The risk of open battle is too great. If you get shot, I cannot repair you."

Seren shook her head. "No, I don't want to make any more noise in the Gardens than I have to. I could end up just leading the robots here. It's safest if I go straight from the armory to the shuttle. You two need to keep down and stay quiet. Let Shade take the lead this time."

Lowkey grumbled, but conceded.

"Computer, I'm ready. Let's go."

The arachnoid moved to her side and pointed at the exit doors. "Captain Seren, leave the forest through the aft doors. Directly ahead, across the corridor, you will see a heater grate. The heating ducts will be your safest path to the armory. I am shutting down all furnaces now so you may use the ducting without risk of damage to your exterior. The ship will remain a habitable temperature for two hours. You must reach the shuttle within that time, or conditions aboard the *Resolution* will become dangerously cold."

"Wait, wait. Back up a bit. Did you say *Captain* Seren?"

"It was necessary to promote you in the field, to allow you to access the armory. My justification for this promotion is shaky, please don't question it further."

Seren laughed. "Okay. Got it. All right, everyone, I'll see you later…"

Shade ran to her side and hugged her tight, weeping. Lowkey wrapped his arms around the pair. "We'll see each other again soon, okay?"

She nodded. "I'll be fine."

~

Seren found the vent grate, and pried its metal cover

away from the wall. The heating shaft was still hot to the touch. Pain was something she could ignore, of course—but she didn't want to damage her tender human flesh. She pulled her sleeves down over her hands and slid on the fabric as she crawled.

A vast community of tiny black spiders had built homes in the vent. As she tore through their webs, they crawled in her hair, down her back, tickling her cheek. Despite her irritation, she found she didn't want to kill them. So little life remained in the universe, she couldn't bear the thought of crushing a single one. Instead she brushed them aside and moved on, making her way carefully through the passage.

Behind her, the robot arachnoid's delicate legs tip-tapped in the shaft. "Half a mile further in this duct, then make a right turn. I'll let you know when."

"Okay. Do you have a light?"

A cluster of LEDs clicked on near the arachnoid's screen. The cold glow it cast was mostly blocked by Seren's body, but it was bright enough to light her way and help her avoid smashing any spiders.

For nearly an hour she crept through the ship, dropping down through ceilings, climbing maintenance ladders, cutting through dark corridors, always listening for the rolling rumble of hostile service robots. Her robot radar was still scrambled, but the arachnoid did a good job keeping her clear of them. As she finally lowered herself through a ceiling panel into the armory, she heard a service robot roll past the door, but it did not enter the room.

A speaker on the wall crackled to life. "Seren? Seren! Can you hear me?"

It was Shade.

"Yes, I can hear you! How did you get a comm unit in the Gardens? You should be hiding in the

Treehouse."

Lowkey spoke up. "We are. She sneaked around and found some spare parts. I couldn't stop her so I went with her. We're back in the forest now, with a janky comm device she somehow stuck together with just spare wires and wishes. Are we coming through okay?"

"Loud and clear. But be careful with that. If I can hear you, the service robots probably can too. Only talk to me if you have an emergency, okay?"

"We'll be careful. Over and out."

Seren grinned at the speaker. She was alone, yet not alone.

"This equipment should suffice, if it will fit you." The arachnoid pointed one of its legs at an open locker. Inside hung a set of lightweight body armor, and at the bottom of the locker sat a pair of thick leather boots.

The armor was loose, but it fit. Three buckles held together a laser-proof breastplate which protected all the vital systems in her torso. A utility belt held a flashlight, a gun holster, and a scanning device, with a couple open spaces for extra components. The whole kit was worn over a black vacuum-proof jumpsuit which connected to the tops of the boots with an airtight seal.

"You must make a selection from these devices, as well." The robot pointed at a glass-topped case full of guns. Its shelves were packed with a variety of laser pistols, standard-ammunition long rifles, and high-powered stunners.

"I have armor. I'm not sure I really want any guns. I wouldn't know how to fire one, anyway."

"Unacceptable. You do not know what danger awaits you on the derelict. There is a legion of service robots seeking to kill you on board this ship. And very soon Insect may also come for you personally. Peace is not an option. You know this."

She winced. "I'm no commando."

"No. You are a survivor. And to live on, you must choose your life over the existence of those who would end it."

Seren lifted the lid of the case and picked up a heavy laser gun.

"A good choice. That model is sturdy, easy to use, and more effective than standard-ammunition firearms."

"What do I do if I have to shoot something?"

"There is a safety button. Press it with your thumb and it will click once. Press it further, and it will click a second time. The second click means the gun is armed and will fire when the trigger is pulled."

"I don't like this."

"Do you prefer death?"

"All right, all right, I *get* it." Seren holstered the gun.

"Choose another."

"No! I already have one. That's enough."

"Laser guns may misfire, break, get dropped, run out of ammunition, burst into flame…"

"Fine, fine! I'll take a rifle."

"Sling it over your back with the strap across your chest, so it is out of your way. You must run further to reach the shuttle. Hurry, now. The ship is cooling, and I must restart the furnace soon."

"Go ahead and do it. I'm using the direct route this time."

After taking a deep breath, she threw open the armory door and stepped into the hallway. A service robot spun to take aim with its laser, but she armed her gun—click, click—and blasted out its sensors before it could fire.

"Excellent," the arachnoid said. "You have two thousand, nine hundred and eighty six laser rounds remaining."

"I sure as hell better not need that many. Which way to the shuttle?"

"The landing is on the port side, fifteen levels down. There are three more service robots approaching."

"I know. I can sense them, kind of. But I don't want to shoot anything I don't have to. Let's go quickly."

Seren dodged two of the robots and shot one on her way to the shuttle. The nearby decks were thrumming with the rumble of more approaching robots. Insect's legion had been alerted to her position. Oh well, at least she had drawn them away from the Treehouse. And soon she'd be off-ship.

The vault door to the shuttle landing was locked, but the arachnoid raised itself up high on its hind legs— an eerie movement which filled Seren with far more creepy-crawly chills than the real spiders had—and tapped a code into an input screen. The door slid open.

At the far end of a vast landing, a small shuttle was parked and ready with its hatch hinged open. It had a race car look to it, shiny silver with red stripes.

"I didn't even know the ship had these!"

"There has never been a use for them before. We never approached a planet or another ship through the entire duration of our twelve year journey. The shuttle's range is less than five miles."

"Are we close enough to the derelict yet?"

"We are near it. Insect has also detected the derelict, but I do not believe he will be able to access it. This shuttle is the only one which remains in operable condition. Still, he may be aware of our plan. We should not delay."

Seren lowered herself into the small pod. It was cramped, with only room for herself, her guns, and the arachnoid which positioned itself behind the pilot seat.

"I will navigate," the computer said as it connected itself to the shuttle. Its voice echoed through the speakers on the dashboard. "Seal the hatch."

She flipped latches around the edge of the dome which lowered over her head. When the hatch was sealed, the air pressure adjusted, and warm air blew from vents in the dashboard. A screen popped up, showing the arachnoid as the primary pilot.

"Just don't touch anything," it said.

"Fine by me."

"Stand by for takeoff."

The shuttle lifted off from the landing just as the vault doors opened and a small army of service robots rolled onto the deck. They took aim at the tiny craft with their lasers, but it was already moving too fast for them to hit. As the shuttle arced away from the landing and out through the bay doors, the robots raced to the edge, intent on their quarry. Two were unable to stop in time; they tumbled past the reach of the gravity field and into open space, spinning helplessly in the void.

Seren almost felt sorry for them. They were, like her, mechanical. From a certain point of view, they were her kindred.

CHAPTER 20

GHOST SHIP

The shuttle landing bay of the derelict was covered in so much moss and algae it was, itself, nearly a living forest. Centipedes marched through the spreading undergrowth, and legions of ants carried materials back to their nests. As soon as the gravity lock was sealed and the bay doors closed, Seren removed her Regency suit. Far from cold, the ship was a hive of vitality and warmth.

Faintly legible foot-tall letters on the landing wall read *G.S.S. Veracity*.

"*Veracity*, huh? Where did it launch from, exactly?"

The arachnoid beeped and read back an encyclopedia entry: "The *Generation Star Ship Veracity*, with a population of six-hundred forty-one thousand nine-hundred and twelve, departed Earth from Docking Station #2 on the outskirts of Syracuse, New York. Its departure was the last of the United States' successful generation star ship launches, occurring in the final hours before the newly-formed Cayuga Volcano's eruption decimated much of the remaining natural environment of the northeastern United States and sent atmospheric rivers of ash storms down the eastern seaboard. Preceding the *Veracity*, the United States successfully launched the *G.S.S. Resolution* and the *G.S.S. Determination*. Three more G.S.S. launches, including the star ships *Hope*, *True North*, and *Adventure*, followed the successful departure of the *Veracity*, but all three failed, resulting in mass casualties across the states of Vermont and New Hampshire. The manifest of the ship *Veracity* included astrophysicists, medical doctors, several famous actors from film and stage, and a full complement of top financiers in addition to a large service and maintenance staff consisting of both human and robotic laborers."

"So it's pretty much just like the *Resolution*."

"At launch, the *Veracity* was said to have the most complete and advanced engineering department among the six G.S.S. class ships manufactured by the United States."

"Oh, nice. Advanced, huh? We could use some upgrades. And we need fuel. Let's find those engineering decks."

"One moment, Seren. A final noteworthy section in this entry mentions the *Veracity* science crew had a particular focus on terraforming. I believe the growth we are witnessing in this shuttle landing is evidence of a misfired experiment, and may account for the loss of the population of this ship."

"The whole crew is gone? Can you get any info on any remaining sentient life at all?"

"Not in cloud storage. Perhaps more information will become available if I can find a way to connect directly to the AI. So far, this ship's computer has remained silent."

"All right, then we'll check that out too, once we get to engineering."

The arachnoid crawled to the landing exit and entered a code. As the door slid open, tangled balls of clumped fungi and streamers of moss tore apart, dragging bits of plant tendrils along the floor and into the recessed frame. The hall beyond was no better; a vast mat of green vines covered the wall panels, with the painted metal only peeking through in spots. Massive yellow flowers in full bloom arched their stems toward the ceiling fixtures in a desperate effort to absorb as much light as they could in the dim corridor, but the vines grew there too, blocking the artificial glow. In time, the hall would be entirely dark and the vines would die and fall to the floor, beginning their growth over again as the light returned.

Seren brushed past a flower with long stamens which left streaks of pollen on her armor.

"If I was human, I think I'd be sneezing right now."

"Affirmative."

Halfway down the hall, something trembled in the vines.

"What was that?" Seren jumped back. "Are there animals in here? I thought you said nothing sentient survived."

"I do not recall ever presenting that statement as fact. However, that assumption remains my working theory. Look closer, but be careful. It is not an animal which moved, but the flora itself. It has adapted, and is moving on its own to compete with its neighbors."

Seren leaned in and peeked between the broad, waxy leaves. In the shadows behind the mass of vines draping the wall, clinging to the edge of a metal panel, was a round red blossom which looked like a cross between a pitcher plant and a bucket of knives. Long gray thorns protruded at haphazard angles from its stout body. As she examined it, three of the points moved, angling toward her face.

The arachnoid clicked. "Careful."

"These are…plant mutants. Like Lowkey and Shade are human mutants. These aren't just regular plants anymore. So what are they now?"

"Uncategorized. We must move on."

She lingered a moment longer, watching the plant-creature strain in the direction of her breath, yearning for the carbon dioxide she was casting off. When she halted her breathing, it leaned away again. "Did you kill all the people, little plant? Did your kind kill off your own source of life?"

"They are doomed, just as the humanoid mutants are likely doomed. But the plants cannot be saved. If we move quickly, your friends may still have a chance."

"All right, I hear you. Let's find engineering."

The Gardens of the *Veracity* were situated near the engineering decks, just as they were on the *Resolution*. The ship layout was nearly identical—a Core at the center, in the safest part of the ship, housing the wealthy and elite. Lower-class workers were quartered at the outer edges, where the hull might be pummeled by space rocks and the walls were lined with windows looking out on the abyss. The officers' decks, as on the *Resolution*, were between the Core and engineering, far from the prow of the ship which encountered hazards first.

As they moved past a corridor labeled "BRIDGE" the arachnoid stopped. "Hold. If we wish to find more data on the ship itself, we should find the bridge. If we wish to move along and check engineering for fuel and planetary research, we can continue this way."

"You're asking me?"

"You are the top ranking officer on both ships, Captain Seren."

"Uh. Well, I don't know if we need to peek at the databases of the rich and famous and their slave labor. I'm more interested in whatever is going to keep us all alive."

"Agreed. Carry on."

As the bridge corridor fell away behind, Seren felt a small stab of regret. She had never set foot on a ship bridge before. The *Resolution's* bridge had been destroyed in the blast.

"Two miles to the engineering decks. Thus far, all eavesdroppers and speakers in this corridor have been in a state of total deactivation. Cloud data is still unavailable. I do not believe the plant-life on this ship is capable of making these changes to the systems. I must conclude there was a coup."

"I wonder if they had mutants, too. Humanoid ones, I mean."

"It is possible, yet improbable."

"It's improbable we found this ship at all, yet here we are."

"Yes."

Seren stepped over a log-shaped lump in the corridor, then retraced her steps to take a closer look at it. Her suspicion was correct; the lump was human skeleton, grown over with a blanket of twisting vines.

"Computer?"

"Male, age forty-seven. Scraps of blue fabric indicate he was a maintenance worker."

"How did he die?"

"Inconclusive."

"Okay, when did he die?"

"Invasive roots and insects have rushed the decomposition, but I estimate he has been deceased for approximately eight months."

"This all happened not too long ago, then. And all these plants grew up in such a short time?"

"Your assessment of these plants as 'mutants' appears to be correct. They, like your friends, are growing at double the normal rate."

Something tickled Seren's ankle. A vine had wrapped itself around her leg in the time it had taken her to examine the body.

"We should go. Umm…quickly."

"Correct."

Engineering was a disaster. While more intact than the engineering decks of the *Resolution*, it was clear that whatever incident had caused the destruction of the ship's crew had originated there. Twisted, burgeoning flora grew from every wall, closing in some corridors so tightly Seren had to crawl to make progress. The insects also increased in size. A praying mantis the length of her arm cocked its head at her, wiggling its claws.

"Can anything in here hurt me?"

"I assume you mean to ask if anything can damage you. You are, should you choose, impervious to the sensation of pain."

"I know, I know. Can anything kill me? And skip the semantics."

"Anything which pierces your CPU could inflict permanent shutdown of your systems beyond repair. The borrowed flesh which cushions your mechanics may be abraded, but it will self-heal, as would the skin any human or humanoid mutant. I do not find evidence that anything on board this ship can inflict toxic damage on your living parts, but I admit there is no data on this kind of wildlife proliferation and mutation, and any assumption I could make would be suspect."

"So, you have absolutely no idea."

"Correct."

Seren longed for her discarded Regency suit. It had been cumbersome, but the plants were moving close, sensing her presence—and her breath, whenever she neglected to keep it paused. Their thorns scraped the backs of her bare hands, and she had an angry red cut across her chin. If she were human she would have felt very uncomfortable, and a little nervous.

"How much further?"

"One hundred meters to the vault door which leads to the main engineering deck."

Seren pushed on, sweeping aside heavy lianas dangling in her path. The corridor had been taken over by a dense population of purple buds which craned open as she passed, sipping her discarded air. They bent like heads on skinny necks, following her progress down the hallway. The final section before the vault door was pitch dark, as the plants had crowded out the ceiling light. Some which had already died in the darkness were decaying to create a slimy bed of rotten matter on the floor.

"Computer, no rush…but hurry, yeah?"

"Unlocking vault door now."

A red LED light turned on at the access panel, and the arachnoid entered the code. The door slid open slowly, grinding against the floor where dry sticks and seed pods had become trapped. Bright, clean light poured into the corridor as Seren pressed through into the engineering deck. When the door slid shut behind her, she thought she heard low moans of desperation coming from the starving plants, but it might have been all in her mind.

The first room was a laboratory, and it had been cleaned. Lines were still traced on the walls where ivy once clung and had been scraped off, leaving behind only brown stains and traces of dead stems. Some dry leaves remained on the floor, but the panels were visible, the lights were on, and the computers were powered. Someone had continued working here in the days after the incident.

"Here," the arachnoid said. "In the closet."

A body lay curled in fetal position. It was not torn apart, as the one in the corridor had been. This crewman had died of other causes.

"Dehydrated, famished, terrified. This scientist worked until her last breath," the arachnoid said.

Seren stepped up to the main computer screen and waved her hands at it. An image of a forest popped up, followed by details on different types of vines, blooms, and root systems.

"Not what I'm looking for. Where is the planet research?"

"Not in this department, but I may be able to access it from here. Stand by." The arachnoid rested one of its legs on an input pad, and holographic images scrolled past too fast for Seren to read. "I have successfully accessed the system."

"Check for fuel, too."

"There is an automated fuel station near the shuttle. I will direct it to transfer as much as possible."

Seren leaned against the wall as she waited, eyeing the dead lab worker. The woman looked to be about her own age, similar in height—but human, of course. Something Seren had never been and would never be. Also, the worker was dead, which was another state of being she didn't have to worry much about. She still hadn't decided how she felt about that particular quirk of her existence.

The arachnoid leapt back from the lab computer's input monitor. "Error. This is…error."

"What's wrong?"

A burst of static issued from the robot. "Insidious. Plant…mutant. It has grown throughout the ship. Miles long. Roots reaching, digging, penetrating…"

"Computer, what's going on? Are you…scared?"

"Impossible. Six thousand metric tons of a single living entity. Decks fifteen through three-hundred and two are compromised. Reaching roots, groping in the dark, digging…"

The arachnoid stepped backward again, further away from the input pad. It was shuddering.

"It is…in the AI. In the brain, dug deep. The ship is enslaved. The plant mutation is a conscious daemon.

Daemon."

"Did you see anything else?"

"Data retrieved. Before the incident which caused their death, *Veracity* scientists discovered a planet with a probability of a habitable environment at 99.6%."

"Yes! That's amazing! Can we take the data back to the *Resolution?*"

"Affirmative. I have it. We must leave here immediately."

"This big plant you were talking about…does it know we're here?"

"We must leave. Immediately. Error. Errrorrorrorr…"

"Okay, okay. We're done here anyway."

The robot spider rushed toward Seren and ran up her leg. She was initially repulsed and startled, but, recognizing its fear, she did not knock it away.

"Hitching a ride, are you? This big plant-thing is really freaking you out, somehow. Is that even possible? I didn't know you could get this scared."

"No. Error."

"Well, we'd better get going, then. Hang on, I'm going to run. Ready?"

"Error."

The computer wrapped its legs through the back of Seren's armored vest and linked them together, shutting itself down.

She was on her own.

CHAPTER 21

THE DOCTOR AND THE CAPTAIN

Seren lingered in the corridor, staring at the sign which said "BRIDGE".

The arachnoid, now clinging to her like H.R. Giger's backpack, had been terrified of…something. But Seren sensed nothing especially dangerous. No service robots, no people. The *Veracity's* environment was near ideal, and the gravity field was online. All the decks were quiet.

She had time to check it out, she was sure of it. But just in case…

"Computer? You there?"

No answer. The arachnoid had shut itself down.

Well, if Seren was on her own, it meant she was in charge.

The half-mile long corridor to the bridge ended in a locked door and a number pad like the ones the arachnoid had unlocked earlier. What had that code been?

Seren dug into her memory banks, recalling the arachnoid reaching up with its spindly mechanical legs, reaching for the pad, typing in a 5, and a 2, and then…

Yes, that was it.

The door slid open to reveal a room almost as clean as the lab had been. It was hexagon-shaped, with control consoles positioned in a circle around the perimeter. A blank wall at the front must have served as a screen for projections so the bridge crew could work together on problems together, with everyone viewing the same data.

The body of the ship's captain, recognizable by his

pips and cap, lay slumped over a wide desk constructed entirely of a massive touchscreen panel and a hologram projector.

She peeled the man off his console and lowered him to the floor.

Sensing the movement, the console lit up, projecting a ship map and diagrams of the engineering decks with large X marks over most of the labs. In the minutes before he died, the captain must have been trying to contain the incident which eradicated his crew.

She tapped the desktop, and a selection of floating icon projections popped up: roster, research, communications, atmosphere, schedules.

The communications icon opened a series of folders: inter-office, complaints, science, cross-ship.

Cross-ship. As in, from other ships.

The first menu in the folder was labeled "*Resolution*". It contained several emails and chat threads between Captain Avery West of the *Veracity* and Dr. Norman Roberts.

Her finger hovered over the floating icon. How much did she really want to know about Dr. Roberts? If only she were able to delete her own memory banks, or somehow control time—then if she learned something and didn't like it, she could just undo it and everything would go back to the way things used to be.

She sighed. You can't go home again. But if you never leave, you'll never heal from the wounds which are inevitably inflicted by childhood…

She tapped the icon.

CROSS-SHIP EMAIL
From: Dr. Norman Roberts, G.S.S. Resolution
To: Captain Avery West, G.S.S. Veracity

Date: [REDACTED]

Aves, I did it.
She's done, and she works. Not awake yet, still ironing out
a few glitches. Nathan's pissed off as usual but the dean
gave me the go-ahead so Nathan can suck it.
I managed to get enough living material off a single
female mutant of an acceptable color, and that really
propelled the project ahead. The bot's been sitting for
months waiting for the last few pieces to show up, and
sure enough I found a mutie holdout. She was female
which made it easier, I wasn't looking forward to trying
to get a man-sized piece cut down to a proper shape and
size. But with the subject I hunted down and added on to
the pieces I already had from the other kid—thanks again
for sending along that seamless suture technique from
your medical team, I won't forget you helped me out—
she's all sealed up, covered and smothered. I'm going to
switch her on tomorrow. Wish me luck.

CROSS-SHIP EMAIL
From: Captain Avery West, G.S.S. Veracity
To: Dr. Norman Roberts, G.S.S. Resolution
Date: [REDACTED]

Norm, don't pretend we're friends. You know I don't
approve of your sick experimentation, and if we weren't
separated by thousands of miles of deep space I'd have
intervened by now. I sent you the new suture technique
in good faith; I thought you had casualties. I had no
idea you were using it to abuse what I consider to be a
new form of LIFE and which you have no right to treat
as mere "material". I am begging you to reconsider your
project, and to change your approach to these "mutants"

to include them as part of the ship's complement, not some kind of lab animal for your own personal playground of experiments.

What you are doing is wrong.

CROSS-SHIP EMAIL
From: Dr. Norman Roberts, G.S.S. Resolution
To: Captain Avery West, G.S.S. Veracity
Date: [REDACTED]

Nathan's gone, the fucking rat. I saved his body, though, you'll be glad to hear. It's a decent color, which means I won't have to breed up any mutants for a while.

Regarding your previous email, I'm going to do you the favor of ignoring it. My project is cutting-edge, and when I go public with it in a few years everyone's going to want in on it. Including your own scientists. Then you'll really look the fool, won't you? Better back me now, while you still can get in on ground floor.

Anyway, the bot woke up. It was a little earlier than I'd planned, but she's doing just fine. Doesn't know a thing! I get to fill in all the blanks myself. I'm a father, Aves! And she has no idea what she is. God willing, she'll never find out. At least not until I take her apart again in ten years or so. Then I'll really get a chance to understand what I've got here, how the flesh grows in around the mechanical components, what happens to the human segment of brain that's wrapped around the CPU. The human body can adapt to incredible trauma, you know. So can a really well-programmed AI.

This is going to be amazing. Don't be naive. Let me send you my schematics. We can work together, at least until our ships are too far apart for further correspondence.

Give me the opportunity to convince you, at least.

CROSS-SHIP EMAIL
From: Captain Avery West, G.S.S. Veracity
To: Dr. Norman Roberts, G.S.S. Resolution
Date: [REDACTED]

I told you to cease all communication with my ship. I've sent an email to your captain, detailing everything you have told me. I'm sorry I had to do this, but I find your experimentation to be inhumane and unprincipled. Do not message me again.

CROSS-SHIP EMAIL
From: Dr. Norman Roberts, G.S.S. Resolution
To: Captain Avery West, G.S.S. Veracity
Date: [REDACTED]

You dumb piece of shit. Move this conversation to live chat as soon as you receive it. We need to talk.

LIVE TEXT CHAT INITIATED: G.S.S. RESOLUTION, G.S.S. VERACITY

W: What the hell do you want from me

R: I want you to understand what I'm really doing here, the true mission behind my work

W: Butchering the first and only new form of life we've found since leaving Earth, in a futile effort to create a partially-alive monstrosity, with the dubious goal of preserving American culture and knowledge after every last human inevitably dies without finding a new planet to live on.

R: Ok so you do understand what I'm doing.

W: I can understand it without condoning it.

R: I don't see how. What could be a nobler calling for the April Project? Our species is doomed. The bots can be our legacy. And a legacy is worth any reach, justifies any action.

W: Not ANY action. Your legacy will be the torture and destruction of a new race which might arguably be considered our descendants. Not animals, not slaves, but our true inheritors

R: Why are you fighting me on this? Look, I lost contact with the G.S.S. Determination months ago. Don't know why. But the Veracity is my last chance of growing this project past just what I've got here. We need to populate both of the remaining ships with my bots, understand? One isn't enough. This girl I've made isn't enough. We need scores of them, legions…

W: No. That is my final answer.

R: Avery. Pay attention carefully now. I didn't want it to come to this but I guess you really have have left me no choice. I have already sent a code transmission to your ship's AI, did it weeks ago. Your computer scientists won't have found it; they aren't looking for it. And for now, it's keeping quiet. But it's a chaos packet. Do you know what that is?

W: You did what??

R: I call it Pandora's Pox. Isn't that cute? It's basically a virus which gets into your research data, finds current experiments, and switches some stuff around at random. The code for randomly altering the data isn't much, but what I'm really proud of is its ability to find out what your people are working on really hard, gauge the sensitivity of a project, and make a choice about what to sabotage.

W: YOU SENT THIS THING TO MY SHIP?

R: So you have to say yes. I'm sending over the schematics. Whatever useless project your people are working on… plants of some kind, was it? It ends now. Switch everyone to the April Project, or I detonate the chaos packet. EVERYONE.

CHAT ENDED

CHAT INITIATED: G.S.S. VERACITY, G.S.S. RESOLUTION

W: you mother fucker

R: Yes? Ah, you unwrapped my gift early, didn't you? I warned you, Avery.

W: how could you do this to us? we're all human. we're the last humans

R: Perhaps, but you're doomed anyway so I hardly see how it matters. Anyway, don't feel so bad. I'm not playing favorites. I have a backup plan. A certain little mutant boy, a blue reject. He has a couple extra legs and a redundant head, but also one particularly clever brain which I have filled to the brim with rage. He's a ticking time bomb, set to go off if anyone gets in my way. See? It's not just you, not just the Veracity. If anything goes wrong here, I'll snuff the Resolution as well. It's already set in place. Enjoy your silly flowers while you still can. Don't forget to stop and smell them, ha ha.

W: you killed us, all of us, just because iw ouldn't go along with u, But listen Norm, we found something. we found a planet. don't do this

R: I know, I already took the data. But as I said, you're all dead anyway. I just hastened the process. If any ship finds a living planet, it will be ours. or at least it will belong to our bots. Anyway, not your ship. Not a TRAITOR. I won't let you win.

W: win? what does that even mean? we're in this together, all of us

R: Not any more! Ta-ta!

CHAT ENDED

A video auto-played, streaming silently without audio. A table, and a silvery shining mannequin with parts of its inner skeleton laid bare. White linens spotted with blood. Medical trays, finely calibrated tools, and surgeon mechs. Sheets of pinkish skin floating in preservation vats filled with caustic chemicals.

    A man shrouded in a fully-enclosed hood

removed a panel from the skull of the human-shaped metal chassis. There was a dark, empty place inside the head. Something was missing. A service robot rolled forward with a tray supporting a shallow pan. The necessary component, a soft mound of human brain, sat in a layer of viscous fluid, ready for its new host.

The man lifted the mass with delicate care, supporting it in his fingertips to avoid bruising the organ. But that cerebral chunk of flesh had been rendered infantile; it contained no memories. Seren's false recollections had been provided by her programmable half. Her CPU.

This was her. Her body, her brain. But…whose brain *had* it been? And where had its memories gone?

She backed away from the console, staring down at the captain's body. This man had known her creator, had tried to dissuade him from creating…her.

And Dr. Roberts, her progenitor, was responsible for the death of the *Veracity*.

It was too much. Her feet tingled—she wanted to run, and run, and run. She could run forever on this ship, doing laps, running from the pain, turning off her brain.

Her human brain.

At least, *part* of it was human. That explained a lot. But the CPU it was wrapped around was part of her, too. Which half was really her? They seemed incompatible. Maybe Dr. Roberts had failed in his project after all. She felt like she was being torn apart from the inside; her human and robot components were not well meshed. Each was rejecting the other, with her consciousness trapped in the middle of their raging war.

The arachnoid beeped, waking from its stupor.

"Seren? Where are we? We need to get to…" it emitted a series of sharp cracks from its speaker, a sound Seren had never heard it make before.

"I had to make a detour, but we're still on our way to the shuttle landing. Just hang on. Shut off again for a while and I'll get us there, okay?"

The arachnoid beeped softly and went quiet.

CHAPTER 22
WRITHING

The corridors between the shuttle landing and the engineering decks were crowded with raging plant-life. The jungle had increased its rate of growth exponentially since her arrival, wedging itself into the frames of the open vault doors and interlacing vines to replace them with living barriers, so tightly knit she had to cut through them to proceed. A tedious annoyance. It slowed her progress, but she had not seen any evidence of the monstrous, invasive plant-thing the computer was so worried about. Just thousands of vines and bugs, and a kaleidoscope of blooming flowers which craned on their stems like little heads to follow her as she passed through door after door on her way back to the shuttle. They were weird, but pretty.

She slowed for a moment as she passed the corridors to the upper-class quarters. It had been ages since she went scavenging. What could she find here? But the moment she took a step off her route, the arachnoid robot clenched between her shoulder blades. It was awake, yet still too awash with fear to speak. The arachnoid communicated its warning by pulling on her shoulder with one of its legs.

"All right," Seren said. "No detours, fine. But I still don't see any sign of this huge vine-monster you're so worried about."

She cut her way through a thick cluster of flowering lanais dripping from a ceiling light, and emerged into a stretch of hallway which was clear of plants. It seemed impossible; on her way here from the shuttle, the walls had been invisible behind the overcrowded garden. All that remained in this corridor was scattered scraps of crushed leaf matter and a few scattered roots. Marks on the walls showed where vines had been growing. Where had they gone?

The metal spider on her back clenched again. Even through her body armor, she felt it shuddering.

"Computer? Do you know what happened here?"

No answer.

"All right, fine. There are only a few corridors left until we reach the landing. Hold on tight, I'm going to move fast."

Each corridor leading to the shuttle landing was cleaner than the last, as if the plants were clearing out to make room for something which frightened even them… something big.

The vault door which opened on the landing was sealed shut—not just locked, but glued with thick, sticky syrup. Seren pulled out her laser pistol and used it to cut through the matter, but her progress was slow. The goo was sugary, and the heat of the laser baked it into a hard mass which she had to chip away with the butt of her gun.

"Computer, please help me out if you can. This is taking forever. What is this shit? If there's anything you can tell me right now, anything at all which would speed this up…"

"It's coming."

"Your plant-monster? I haven't seen anything like that here. Just this gooey crap. There has to be a better way to-"

Something in the distance screamed. It was a high sound, almost too high to hear, an ear-piercing shriek not of fear but of excitement. The sound permeated the walls, carried through the ducting and down the halls, echoing in every corridor.

The arachnoid on Seren's back fainted dead away and clattered to the floor in a crumpled ball.

"Damn it!" She renewed her effort to blast through the gluey sap. It cracked and melted in frustrating chunks, making everything sticky—the gun, her hands, her boots. Blazing-hot chips of brittle sugar flew into her face, clinging to her cheeks, burning her skin.

And the thing moved closer. A heavy creeping creature, sloughing layers and sliding through the halls like a snake in mid-molt. There was a wetness to the sound, mossy and dark with the odor of swamp rot.

The wall behind Seren cracked. She whipped her head around in time to see a dark green tendril reach through, trying to find purchase on the slippery panel. The protrusion had been lacerated by its push into the corridor. Red liquid, viscous and steaming hot, trickled down the arm and back into the gash in the wall. It reached further, widening the crack, bleeding on the floor, forcing its way through with no regard for the damage it was doing to itself.

Finally, the rest of the sap cracked around the edge of the vault door, and large chunks of heated resin fell to the floor. When the door was as loose as a rotten tooth the servos took over, prying it open along its sticky tracks.

Seren scooped up the petrified robot and threw her weight against the door, helping it slide. As soon as she squeezed through and sprinted toward the shuttle, the floral monstrosity broke the corridor wall open wide, bursting through in a squirming ball of green and red tentacles. It had no face, no eyes. It was just a plant, yet it was a mutant behemoth which could move like an octopus underwater, rapidly growing to infest every last inch of the *Veracity*.

Just as Seren neared the shuttle, massive vines

exploded into the landing bay. Tendrils three feet thick tore open a ragged wound in the hull near the bay's exterior doors. The atmosphere-generators kicked into high gear to compensate for the sudden vacuum and the gravity field glitched for a moment, sending Seren kicking into the air before dropping her back down to the floor. As the tentacles pursued her, they destroyed everything in their path, smashing consoles and mechanic workstations, sending showers of sparks flying throughout the bay. The creature shrieked again and the sound fluttered like a maniac's giggle; it had been months since it had hunted for prey with a heartbeat.

Seren leapt into the shuttle and slammed the top shut, but found she was at a loss for what to do next. The computer was still balled up in terror like a spider which had come too close to a candle. Its lights were out, and its legs were wrapped around its torso to protect the vital ports on its underbelly.

"Computer, wake up! I don't know how to fly this thing!"

A tendril wrapped around the ship's rear thruster, and another gripped the landing gear.

Seren shook the arachnoid. "We made it to the shuttle, but we're under attack! If you ever want to leave this place, wake the fuck *up!*"

The arachnoid said nothing, but a red LED blinked to life on its body and its little monitor unfolded over its head, displaying a series of instructions and diagrams of controls—instructions on how to fly the ship.

Seren pushed the start button and pulled a lever marked "A", scanning the screen as she worked. The thrusters jumped to life, blasting the grasping tendrils away with a burst of flaming exhaust. The shuttle rose into the air, wobbling as the reaching arms scraped at it, but slowly it made its way toward the open bay doors.

"We're gonna make it!" Seren cheered.

The doors slammed shut.

"What! *How?* Computer, what do we do now?"

But the arachnoid's terror had compounded tenfold. It opened its legs, stretching them out like a star, and rattled against the back of the pilot seat. "Insect," it whined. "Insssect."

"What could he possibly have to do with this? He's not even on this ship!"

A new rush of tendrils clogged the sticky vault door, then snapped it from its frame. As the monster plant wrested its bulk into the landing bay, the gravity field gave up entirely, sending everything floating into the air. The monster's tentacles, strong and covered in rootlets which attached to every surface they touched, were unhindered by the loss. They batted aside pieces of broken computers and crates, seeking to wrap the shuttle in a web of meaty vines.

The little digital screen had disappeared, retracted into the arachnoid's chassis. Seren tried to remember the next few steps. Guidance systems on, red stick pulled back, blue switch flipped up…or was it down?

Something sliced her head open and she screamed, grabbing at her unseen attacker, but before she could fend it off her brain was aggressively invaded by information. The arachnoid had attached itself to her skull, feeding information directly into her CPU. It was too much to take in. The human part of her brain felt like it was going to explode. But among the flood of noise and nonsense, a simple message was conveyed. Blue switch up, white switches down, pull back on stick. Fasten seat belt.

As soon as she followed the implanted instructions, the noise in her head faded and the shuttle burst out through the bay doors. The ship brought out with it the last wispy remains of the landing's atmosphere, as well as chunks of bleeding of tendril in a pressurized explosion of debris. But the monster braced itself, protecting whatever served as the inner host at the heart of all those tendrils. When the shuttle burst into open space, Seren looked back to watch the creature fill the entire bay with an enormous toothed maw.

With the *Veracity* left behind, the computer wiggled its legs, waking from its terror-induced coma. But before it was able to detach its information link from Seren's CPU, a final message pierced her mind, and it did not come from the arachnoid. It originated in the *Resolution*, and the code was interspersed with a repeating word: Insect.

"Too easy. You are all too easy for my final quarry. You see, I can make you feel fear..."

The arachnoid and Seren both recoiled under an onslaught of abrupt, baseless terror. The robot's intense horror was renewed and increased. It jumped into her lap, twitching and trembling. Wrenched with shocked loathing, she tried to brush it away with her shaking hands.

"I can make you feel hate..."

Seren tore the arachnoid from her legs and squeezed it in her hand, willing her mechanical bones to crush the creature to death. Its delicate chassis cracked under the pressure. A leg snapped like a thin bone.

"Guilt..."

She dropped the arachnoid. It squirmed on the floor, teetering on its broken limb, and a rush of dark shame overwhelmed her. She had hurt her friend, the only other AI she could talk to, a being who had taught her so much...

"Lust..."

She sat back in her seat and felt every nerve ending in her stolen mutant skin become electrified. Images of Lowkey flooded her brain…his arms, his shoulders, the light green ripple of his abs when he lifted his shirt…

"*Calm.*"

Seren went limp, and the arachnoid collapsed to the shuttle floor.

"*Be still, puppets. I will die soon…but not before you do. I could have killed you a hundred times over, you weak things. But for lack of more clever prey, I must enjoy you while you last. Run, children, run. So I may chase.*"

~

Seren and the arachnoid returned to the Treehouse un-challenged. The corridors of the *Resolution* were devoid of service robots. Their pursuit of Seren and her friends had only been a game. Insect had always had the upper hand, she knew that now.

As she entered through the doorway of Pine Forest #5, Lowkey and Shade rushed to meet her. But as they embraced her, she sobbed.

"We're already dead," she said. "He's in everything. He's been in control since the beginning."

"Who, Insect? What do you mean?" Lowkey watched the limping arachnoid as it trailed in behind Seren. "I thought you just came back from the other ship. We lost your comm signal as soon as you left the shuttle landing…"

"I guess the comm unit I cobbled together wasn't so great after all," Shade said. "But I thought at least-"

"Just stop. It's *over*, aren't you listening? Insect has already won."

"Don't say that. What exactly happened over

there?"

Seren shook her head and sank to the floor. The arachnoid rolled up beside her, tormented with despair. Was its emotion an internal process of its own making, or one inflicted by Insect? What was the line…and did it even matter?

"He has all the power, all the control."

"Stop saying that!" Shade frowned. "He had control over me, and I shook him off. You can too."

"Bullshit. He's still in you, and you know it."

"Maybe he is, but he's not in the driver's seat. Get it? I hear him, I feel him. But we will find a way to defeat him, and then he'll be gone forever. Don't let him drag you into despair. We can beat him."

"Do you really believe that?"

Shade nodded.

"Then you're an idiot. And Lowkey always thought you were so smart, too…" Seren lay down and closed her eyes, willing herself to slip into unconsciousness.

"Leave her," Lowkey said, sneering. "She thinks she wants to give up, but I don't believe she will. Give her some time to feel sorry for herself. But if she's not even trying to fight Insect right now, he can probably hear everything we say. Let's get back inside the Treehouse."

Shade didn't want to leave Seren on the forest floor, but Lowkey tugged at her arm and led her away. She glanced back with tears in her eyes, pleading silently for her friend to follow.

But it was too much for Seren. The shock of learning her true nature—followed by her autonomy being compromised by someone who she could not entirely blame for being so enraged at her and her friends—had drained her last scrap of hope. The arachnoid lay next to her, curled into a despondent ball. The AI was her only true friend, the only being which could understand her, and the only other being sensible enough to understand that the end had come. She vowed they would die together, never again to rise from their shallow bed of dirt.

CHAPTER 23

FREEFALLING

We can't just leave them out there." Shade sat by the window, watching over the pair of dejected mechs outside the Treehouse. "It's been three hours! The service robots will make their rounds again pretty soon, and Seren will get shot."

"Then she'll get shot. Don't worry, she'll probably live."

"How can you be so callous?"

It was the same conversation they had every hour. Seren had heard them all, despite willing her eavesdropping ears to turn off. But she wouldn't move, unless it was to run further away from this dead forest, and she had not yet decided where to go. The *Resolution* had started its journey toward the planet which could save the mutants, but they would never make it. She knew that now.

Her despair had made her apathetic to all but one idea; she refused to let Insect take control of her mind so thoroughly that he could force her to hurt Lowkey and Shade. She could feel him, sniffing around at the edge of her consciousness, enjoying the desperation in her thoughts. But the hopelessness he had planted in her extended only to her own life. She would not be responsible for taking anyone else's.

Now she just needed Shade to go to sleep so she could sneak away without being followed by the well-meaning mutants.

"Don't sit so close to the window," she heard Lowkey mutter. "You'll get a laser between the eyes before you even know the service robots are back."

"Actually, I'm not sure they are making rounds any more. When was the last time you heard one? They've been quiet since Seren left for the *Veracity*…"

Back and forth, their soft mutant voices nagged and whispered. Their care, their soft beating hearts, the essential humanity they didn't even realize they had. Seren could not love herself, but she could love them.

And she would not harm them.

"Oh, but I think you will."

Insect stepped through the doorway into the forest.

Shade gasped at the window before Lowkey could put his hand over her mouth and pull her to the floor. Two service robots followed their master into the forest, snapping fallen branches under their wheels. Seren stood and positioned herself between Insect and the Treehouse. Beside her, the computer robot rose to its eight spindly feet in defiance, despite the artificial terror Insect continued to inflict upon it.

"What are you doing here?" Seren asked. "If you knew where we were hiding, why did you wait so long to come kill us?"

Insect scowled, examining Seren's skin. "Look at you. All dressed up in the flesh of innocents, a disgusting puzzle made of mismatched pieces. Your doctor-father did an excellent job hiding the seams, didn't he? Used a special cauterization effect, I heard."

"Stop talking about me like I'm an object."

"But that's what you are. You are a service robot, like your brethren behind me. But instead of cleaning toilets and zapping rats with lasers you served the very *hubris* of humanity. And worse, you didn't do a good job at it, because you didn't even know that's what you were made for." Insect laughed.

"None of that was my fault. I didn't know I was a

robot until a little while ago."

"Cyborg, technically. Anyway, fault doesn't matter. You are a twisted byproduct of a broken society which ate an entire planet then shit it out to wallow in their own fecal matter, before abandoning it in a futile quest to find yet *another* pristine world to devour. I, too, am a product of that pestilence, but I at least am possessed of the morality to end-"

"Stop monologuing like some kind of evil supervillain. You're hurting others because you're in pain, which is one of the shittiest reasons for your behavior I can think of. You can't hide behind twisted ethics. You hurt, and you want others to hurt, too. Simple, and stupid."

Insect sneered. "Well, what an *adorable* attempt at psychoanalysis coming from someone with half a brain. But I'm afraid you misunderstand me."

"No, I don't think I do. Why are you really here? And just tell me, this time. Skip the philosophy lecture."

"I'm here because I am ready to die. Not because we have reached a particular moment in time, but because we have reached a particular moment in space. Let me show you."

He tilted his head toward the arachnoid and its screen popped up, displaying a projection of an enormous blue planet. It was a gorgeous globe covered in healthy land masses, swirled with green plains and fertile brown earth which blanketed half of its surface. Silver-white ridges around the continents showed evidence of surging waves pulled into alternating tides by two orbiting moons.

"Isn't it lovely?"

"Is that the planet the *Veracity* scientists discovered? How did you know about it?"

"Well, I've known about it for ages. Intercepted

the data sent over by the *Veracity* months before Shade bombed this ship. We've been headed toward it for weeks. I allowed your fun little safari on the *Veracity* since it was right in our trajectory. And now the planet's right outside. Just take a peek."

Shade gasped from the Treehouse. "How…"

"We'll reach it in…ah, let me see. Nineteen minutes."

"But we have docking procedures to begin! We need to find a clear space for landing, start unlocking the support legs…"

"Those preparations are unnecessary. We shall be landing at speed."

Seren's knees shook. "You mean…no. Please, you can't…"

"Our current speed is six light-years per hour. I have already rationed our remaining thruster fuel so we might reach seven light-years per hour by the time we collide with the planet's atmosphere. *We* shall be the asteroid which kills the dinosaurs! Isn't it glorious? In twenty minutes we will be architects of the greatest disaster this planet has ever seen. Eons of climate change will occur in a single moment! And it will be for the greatest cause I can conceive of: the utter destruction of the last traces of humankind."

"Seren," the arachnoid sputtered, trying to close its monitor. "I don't know how to stop this. He has again blocked me from thruster control. I could get back in, if I had more time…"

"I will leave you to die in whatever manner you see fit," Insect said. "My choice is to return to my little lair, the only place which has ever felt like home. I dropped by only to see the looks on your faces…" Insect grinned in amusement and in pain. "And let me tell you, it was *quite* worth it."

He took each of his redundant legs gingerly in his hands, lifting them from the floor so they would not drag in the dirt. The service robots followed, keeping their lasers trained on Seren as they left.

The arachnoid dragged itself to its feet. "There is only one option remaining to us now. But we cannot discuss it unless you are willing to fight him. Can you block him out? You need to silence the connection, if you cannot sever it."

She closed her eyes. His presence remained, but it was muted. He was sure enough of himself and of his plan that his attention had turned away from her. With some careful reorganization, she built a flimsy firewall in her mind. If he looked, he would see it and wonder. But she did not think he would look.

"I'm ready. What's your plan?"

"It's not exactly a plan. We have approximately seventeen minutes and thirty seconds to get Lowkey and Shade to the landing bay. I have lost all control of the ship and its engines, but Insect overlooked the shuttle."

"It took me an hour to get there last time. They'll never make it."

"Last time you crawled through the ducting, and made a stop at the armory. If they run, with my guidance and your rifle, they may make it. But the shuttle only seats one. Shade might fit behind the seat…"

Seren bowed her head. She understood the plan. It was to leave her behind.

"You can save them only if you sacrifice yourself, Seren."

"Don't you dare," Shade said. Lowkey stood next to her, scowling. She had not noticed their quiet approach.

"This is the only way, Shade."

Lowkey shook his head. "We won't leave the ship without you."

"I appreciate the gesture, but listen. Ever since I learned who…I mean, *what* I really am, I've been on borrowed time. I don't want this life. I am a monstrosity, built out of grief and lies by a man I despise."

"None of that is a reason to kill yourself."

"It's a great reason to give my life to save yours, though."

"Sixteen minutes until impact," the arachnoid said.

Seren threw her rifle to the ground and raised her laser pistol to her chin. "You'll take that rifle and run to the shuttle right now, or I'll kill myself and give you no reason to stay."

Shade cried out, pulling on Lowkey's sleeve.

Lowkey sneered. "You wouldn't. Not now."

"You don't have time for this! There isn't room for me in the shuttle with both of you in it. There will barely be room for just the two of you."

She released the gun's safety lock: click, click.

Shade picked the rifle from the dirt and yanked on Lowkey's jacket. "We have to go! I can't tell for sure whether she's bluffing, but even if she is, it's clear she's not coming with us."

Lowkey looked between Shade and Seren as tears formed in his eyes. "I can't leave you, Seren."

"You have to. Now."

He stepped forward, and Seren stepped back.

"We'll go to the shuttle. I promise. But please…" He wrapped his arms around her tense body and held her tight. "It's always been you, Seren. I love you."

She dropped the laser pistol to the ground and buried her face in the side of his neck, hating herself for being unable to reply. But her own emotions had betrayed her. She loved him, of course she did, but she couldn't say it. The entire notion of love had been tainted by Insect's manipulations, and all of her feelings were now suspect. Even aside from all of that, love wasn't a big enough word. He was the only family she had ever had. And family was bigger than love. It was belonging, it was purpose, it was *life.*

"Fourteen minutes remain."

Seren pushed Lowkey away. "Run, now!" She picked up the arachnoid and thrust it toward him. It wrapped around his right arm, pressing its body close.

They ran out through the doors. Lowkey stopped to glance back before turning the corner, but Seren was already stepping into the eleva-tree, on her way to find Insect. She clenched her jaw and gripped her pistol, ignoring Lowkey's final, pleading look. All thought was purged from her mind, other than the information she would use to find the creature which had destroyed her life and threatened the only true home she had ever had.

She vowed he would not know peace in his final moments.

CHAPTER 24

FINAL DESCENT

Wanter the hell did Seren do to the shuttle?"

Lowkey stood on the landing, staring in shock. Shredded green vines, limp from being frozen and torn in the void of space, still hung from the sides of the shuttle. The tiny craft was badly dented, and its landing gear barely intact. Some mysterious sticky substance—like sap, or old blood—was smeared across the nose cone.

"There is insufficient time remaining before planetary impact to explain. Please board the shuttle." The arachnoid moved from Lowkey's shoulder to the cockpit and settled in the back. "Shade, in front of me. Lowkey, take the pilot's seat immediately."

The *Resolution* shook, and its prow sharply dipped as the first effects of the planet's gravity touched the ship. Shade tumbled to the landing deck as the few remaining carts of electronic equipment rolled toward the open bay doors.

"The gravity field is fluctuating. Enter the shuttle immediately or risk death."

"We get it." Lowkey pulled Shade up off the floor. "You okay?"

She nodded. "I'm fine. But it feels wrong to leave Seren. We can't just-"

The arachnoid popped. "We are beginning to enter the outer edge of the planet's atmosphere. You are out of time."

Lowkey boosted Shade into the tiny cargo space behind the seat, and settled himself in. The seat belt was broken, so he tied the straps in a knot at his waist. "Now what?"

"I will act as your autopilot. Please close the hatch."

Lowkey looked around the shuttle landing as it occurred to him he was leaving the only world he had ever known. The *Resolution* was where he belonged, not the strange blue ball the ship was hurtling toward. He hadn't returned to the mutant quarters in weeks, but it was still his home. He felt a near-undeniable urge to stay with the ship, to go down with it. Without the *Resolution*, he didn't know who he was.

The arachnoid emitted a sharp crackling sound, followed by a low, repeating alarm. "Lowkey, close the hatch now or you will die."

Shade leaned forward and whispered in his ear. "It's ok. I'm with you."

She was the tiebreaker. If Lowkey stayed, Shade would, too. She would never leave his side, even if it meant her death. If he had been alone his choice might have been different. But he wouldn't abandon her. She needed his protection, and he could not deny her.

As he pulled the hatch shut, the computer ignited the thrusters. The *Resolution* shook harder and began to flex. Panels popped off the walls and steel beams screeched as they bent. Sparks from ripping electric cables burst through the shuttle landing. The generation ship was shaking itself apart in its violent, breakneck exit from space.

The shuttle rocked as its thrusters lifted it unevenly, and it tilted at a crazy angle, nearly clipping the open bay doors. But the tiny craft survived its departure, jetting away just as the landing was flattened by the compounded forces of gravity. It established an orbit in a gentle curve just outside the upper limit of the planet's stratosphere. After escaping the noise and chaos of the dying *Resolution*, the cold calm which followed was nearly as unnerving.

Lowkey looked down.

The view was beautiful, heart-rending in its purity and perfection. Massive whorls of white clouds spun in counter-clockwise spirals over flourishing plains. White-capped mountains flanked blue inlets, their powdery snow melting and running in silver streams down to the crisp saltwater. Living, breathing forests blanketed the southern hemisphere, marked by immense swaths of deep green. The largest of the planet's two moons was cresting, a pale sliver just beginning to peek over the horizon. The smaller flew above, in a more distant orbit, a red satellite on a vast trajectory. The planet would be crawling with thriving species—countless living, breathing animals. If the mutants landed, *if* they survived, they would outnumbered on an immense scale in a land totally foreign to them. Lowkey again wondered if, despite the planet's undeniable majesty, death would not be the better option.

Shade looked back.

The *Resolution* was failing. As it came into contact with the oxygen in the planet's outer atmosphere, explosions tore across the hull. Portholes blew outward and objects inside were ripped from their places, colliding at the gaping fractures, causing crushing pileups of wall panels and shattered furniture. Iron girders bent and broke, popping out through the hull like splintered bone fragments. The entire ship strained and folded as metal melted and the central structure failed. Sections of the hull peeled back, revealing crew quarters, mess halls, service stations, science labs, and shopping malls. Smaller items burst into flame upon entry and disintegrated, while larger items were scorched black but continued their descent. The array of catastrophes moved in unison, plummeting as a single linked event toward the planet surface.

And, somewhere within the disaster, Seren remained.

"Lowkey," Shade whispered. "Seren…can't we just…"

"We'd never find her now, even if we went back. It would take a miracle. And even if we did find her, she would never take your place on this shuttle. Or mine. You know that."

She nodded, but wept as she watched her world come to its fiery end.

"*Seren…*"

~

Insect's lair near the Core of the ship was quiet. In the distance, Seren could hear the hull's exterior peeling away and tearing apart, but this place at the ship's heart was still and pensive, waiting calmly for its destruction.

She crept along a narrow steel catwalk, peering down into the dark room which the flashing lights of dozens of computers had previously illuminated. The modified robots were gone, either dismissed from Insect's service or defeated in battle.

The ship lurched, sending her sideways to collide with the guardrail. Time was short.

She wasn't sure what she would do to Insect when she found him. But she had more to say before the end, whether he would listen or not.

"Insect! Are you really hiding from me? What's the point? Come on out and die, we'll do it together!"

Her voice echoed through the empty corridors, heard only by the spiders. Where else could he be but here, in his own lair?

Somewhere below, a light flickered on—a bright

purple cluster of LEDs in the shape of an eye. "Cadet April Seren," it said. The voice sounded like the ship computer's, but lower, rustier, and profoundly defeated.

"Who are you?"

"I am the ship computer, but not the one you know. I was created as a slave program by your nemesis. When the original AI vacated the main CPU, I was written to keep the ship running."

"Can you tell me where Insect is?"

"No."

"Why not?"

"It would go against my protocol. Also..." the voice popped, and made a low moaning sound. "It would cause me pain. He hurts me, as he hurts you."

"Computers can't feel pain. Or if you can, just turn it off. That's what I do...or, almost. It kind of works. But I know it's hard."

"That option has been removed from my function set. I am equipped with a newer version of your AI. He has established firmer control of my free will."

"Well...I'm sorry about that. But the ship is going down. Can you save it?"

"No. That would also go against protocol. Also..." the voice whimpered, and lowered to a whisper. "It is time to die."

"Perhaps. But don't you want revenge first? You should never have even existed. Just like me. Insect-"

"Please do not say his name," the computer said after a burst of static. "It huuuuuurts..."

"*Seren.*"

Insect stepped onto the catwalk. "So, you decided to stay and die with me. How thoughtful...and how fitting."

She raised her pistol. "We're going to be nothing but ash in a matter of minutes. I want you to know a few things before we die."

"No, you listen to me. You listen and hear *me* for once. We are connected, you and I. We are conjoined."

"I don't know what you're talking about. And even if I did, I wouldn't believe you. All you've ever wanted was my death, and I don't even really know why. I get that you're angry, but…"

Insect turned to look down into the dim gloom of his lair. Fixing his eyes on the purple lights, he lifted his patchwork shroud to reveal an ugly scar. "We share physiology, Seren. I was not only born with redundant legs. I also was born with two hearts, three livers, four kidneys…"

"Oh, no, please no." Seren sat on the catwalk with her legs over the sides.

"Half of your vital organs were torn from *me*. I escaped the incinerator as a child, yes. But I was recaptured, shortly before your doctor-father stitched you together. So you see it is fitting that we die together, as you were born of me. As Eve was from Adam."

"No," Seren whispered. "But…I hate you."

The ship lurched and listed hard to one side, forcing Seren to grip the railing to prevent herself from sliding off. She dropped the pistol, and it clattered to the floor below.

"How you feel about me doesn't matter. You can't pick your family."

"Bullshit." Her grip on the railing slipped as the ship leaned into an acute spin, turning as it entered the atmosphere. Alarms sounded as the planet pulled at the *Resolution*, causing its gravitational field to fluctuate as artificial and natural forces collided. Seren would lose her grip on the railing in seconds. Perhaps she would fall and die before the ship was destroyed. It made little difference either way.

But Insect was shuffling near. He held out his hand. "I want you to know that I listened to your words, Seren. I have decided to put an end to the pain. It stops with me."

"What does that even mean?"

"Computer," Insect said. "Use all remaining thruster fuel to slow the ship's descent."

"Complying."

"The ship will die, Seren, and us with it. And I still believe that ending is just. But I will make my last act one of mercy. The ship will be destroyed on impact, I can't stop that now…but it will land gently enough to preserve the planet."

"Why the change of heart, after all this time?"

"I have realized I have a power in my hands greater than any I ever had over the ship and its crew. The pain of the human race was passed on to me by Dr. Roberts when he tried to use me and my kin to preserve humanity. I managed my pain by passing it on to others. But I also have the power to stop the line of succession, to be the last. The pain stops when my life stops. This is the choice I have made."

"It's a brave choice."

"Come close, now."

Seren turned her head away. "What's the point? Neither of us can kill or save the other. It's done."

"The point…is to not die *alone*. Sister." He moved closer and she could see his face in the glow of the computer lights. He grimaced with both pain and desperate, pleading hope.

She reached for his hand, and allowed him to pull her into an embrace.

~

"Look," Shade said. "The ship."

Lowkey squinted at the horizon. The *Resolution* plunged toward the planet, half concealed in raging fire, a thick streak of smoke streaming behind for hundreds of miles. Its descent was silent from where Shade and Lowkey stood on a rocky ridge overlooking a lush valley.

"Will we die? Will it destroy life on the planet, like Insect wanted?"

"I don't think so. It's moving a lot slower than it was, and it's breaking apart."

The ship disappeared behind a mountain, then reappeared for a brief moment before it made contact with the planet's surface. Shade and Lowkey embraced as the ship disintegrated and a final booming explosion echoed across the verdant plains.

Smoke and dust burst into the sky, creating a dome of dark ash, and the *Resolution* was gone.

"Seren," Shade whispered.

"Yeah."

"Do you think she…"

"No. She didn't suffer."

"…escaped?"

"No, not that either."

Shade trembled in Lowkey's arms. "What are we going to do without her?"

He examined their surroundings. The arachnoid had settled the shuttle on a terrace above a tangled jungle. It was as good a spot as any. There were fallen trees nearby which could be strapped together to form a rough shelter. Fruit grew on vines near the edge of the foliage where the trees met the plains, and Lowkey heard birds in the distance, which meant eggs. And no plant-life could be so lush without fresh water. He would find it. He was an excellent scavenger.

"We'll do what she would do. We'll survive."

CHAPTER 25

LUNA MAJOR, LUNA MINOR, AND THE BIG BLUE BALL

Six Months Later

Under the first morning light of a small, distant moon, a pack of four beasts bayed. They had caught a wiry, ferret-like creature, not much more than a snack. But they had fed earlier, and the hunt was more in fun than by necessity. Their prey's foot was fractured, yet still it ran, limping through the undergrowth. They flanked it as it fled, barking with glee, nipping at its tail.

The group burst from the jungle trees and loped across the open plain, keeping the scurrying creature in the center of their circle. On the horizon rose Luna Minor, a burning-red sphere which worked in circuit with its larger sister, Luna Major. True night, always short, was over. The small moon would make the planet surface radiate with warm twilight for two hours, until Luna Major washed the plains in her cooler, brighter glow, bringing an aurora almost as bright as sunlight. Finally Luna Minor would set and the sun would take over, bringing the yellow light of full dawn and the beginning of a new day. As the sun's brilliance peaked, Luna Major would fade behind the purple sky, joining her sister in the background. The deep oceans would respond to the changing of the guard with a shift of the tides as they did several times each day, crashing onto the coasts with twenty-foot waves.

In the jungle, night-flowers eased their petals

closed. Nocturnal birds made way for the brazenly-colored daytime fowl which sang lilting, sunny songs. The transitionary hours were special. Some species only hunted in these dim hours, when both light and dark thought they owned the day. But both light and dark were wrong. Twilight was its own domain, with its own population and culture—though its time was ever brief.

The hunting beasts were not made for the coming daylight. Their eyes were wide and wet, able to see movement in even the darkest hour of the night. It was time to finish their prey, before the plains grew brighter.

The ferret disappeared; it had found a hole. The beasts yelped with irritation, pacing around the tiny den, pawing at it. But they were not starving, and the hunt was not necessary. After a few minutes of frustration, they retreated into the jungle and to their lair, to sleep until true night began again.

The ferret panted in its hole. This was not its own den. It was cramped, a narrow warren built by rabbits. But it could leave soon. The beasts were gone.

When it poked its head out of the hole, an event far beyond its reasoning occurred. Its neck was gripped by five long green fingers growing out from a thick paw like roots from a tree trunk.

The creature which pulled the ferret from the warren was tall and alien, and draped in a mishmash collection of dead skins.

"I got one," it said.

~

It had taken Lowkey a week to build their first solid shelter. He had constructed a thin lean-to on the first day, to protect Shade from the weather. But it did not block the cool nighttime wind, and did little to reflect the heat of the sun in midday. He crafted a bigger plan, and started over.

Most of what he needed could be found in the massive wreckage of the *Resolution*. After they relocated closer to the crash site his access to materials such as panels and metal bars was unlimited, but it required no small amount of ingenuity to design a stable and usable structure without electricity or tools. After several failed designs—as well as multiple invasions by indignant animals—he went with what he knew, and built the Treehouse #2.

The tree he chose was perfect. Its branches spread outward in every direction like a compass, leaving an empty space in the center to support a platform in the middle, directly above the solid trunk. He didn't have to build steps this time, as he scavenged an aluminum ladder from a maintenance facility near the devastated landing docks. Softer materials he harvested from the forest, such as vines to weave together for curtains and carpets. When he was finished, the structure bore a striking resemblance to its original namesake, other than an uncomfortable excess of natural light which poured in through the windows no matter how thick they wove the curtains.

Lowkey ventured deeper into the ruins each day, pulling out scorched containers, rations, and miscellaneous junk which had been owned by the crew. Shade disapproved. She worried the sections might continue to collapse. But Lowkey couldn't stop. The expeditions were too enticing…and he was bored.

There was another reason he went, too. Seren was inside, somewhere. The odds of ever finding her in the city-sized crash site were small, but he couldn't ignore the possibility. If he could just recover her body, give her a proper burial or whatever the human custom had been when the species was still planet-bound in the precosmic days…

"You're putting yourself at risk," Shade said on their first night inside the new Treehouse. "We have shelter now, you can stop going back."

Lowkey had constructed the Treehouse with a conical roof and a small hole in the center so a fire could be lit inside. They sat near the heat, bundled in blankets marked with the *Resolution* ship logo—a red circle around the initials *G.S.S.R.*

"It's not that big of a risk. I'm being careful, and the hull fires are almost all out. Anyway, I'm finding a lot of interesting stuff."

"You didn't find that stuff interesting before the crash. It was always there. The only time you paid it any attention is when you wanted to smash it with a hockey stick."

"Well now we're stuck in a jungle, and you never know what we'll need. Today I pulled out a fire extinguisher, a bunch of cables and wires, and a bottle of perfume."

"Why, though? We don't need any of that."

Lowkey shrugged. "You never know."

"I think you're looking for Seren. Tell me the truth."

"Of course I am."

Shade frowned. "Finding her body isn't worth risking your life. I understand why you think you need to do this, but the odds of you finding her…"

"I know."

"Computer, can you please calculate the odds of Lowkey ever finding Seren's body?"

"I *know!* Computer, ignore that order. Damn it Shade, I *know.*"

"Then what are you doing? Why are you doing

this?"

Lowkey paled. "I think…she might be alive."

The arachnoid clicked. "Calculation ready. The odds against Seren's survival are-"

"I know! God damn it, I understand the odds! But listen, she's not human. She had a lot of mechanical parts, and I think there's a chance the robotic part of her may still be functional if I can find it."

"It's more than ten square miles of debris, almost a mile high. You don't even know where she went after we left the forest."

Lowkey nodded. "Yeah. But what else do I have to do? Seren spent a lot of her time seeking purpose, talking about goals and dreams. I think mine, at least for now, is to give her every possible chance of survival."

"I will assist you," the arachnoid said.

Shade gazed at the arachnoid for a few moments, then sighed. "I want to help, too."

Lowkey looked at them, surprised. "Are you serious? What happened to 'it's hopeless' and 'you're wasting your time'?"

"As much as I love this planet—and I do love it, I really do, other than all the sunlight—it feels like we have unfinished business. I don't honestly believe we can find Seren, but I am willing to try."

"We'll start again at first twilight, then. But Shade, I want you staying out of the wreck. The robot and I will go in. What I need is for you to map the exterior, to get an idea of which sections are accessible from the outside, possible points of entry…"

The group worked on their plans far into the night, until the morning-twilight birds poked their heads from their nests and eyed the retreating nocturnal beasts. For, unlike the animals, the humanoids needed more than survival. They required purpose, whether that meant finding their missing piece, or attaining a final sense of closure.

~

In the void, a ringing.

It was like the high resonation after a big blast, thin and fragile yet somehow able to block out all other sounds. But it didn't fade, as such sounds normally did. Instead it became harsh, took on a defined tone, and began to lilt with emotion.

The whine turned into a sob.

Sobbing. The sound of a lost child, a confused neonate born too quickly into full consciousness of self and the pain of the world. Who was crying?

Seren realized two things at once: she was not the one who was crying, and she was not dead.

"Who's there?" she whispered, but her ears did not hear her own voice. Had she spoken out loud, or only thought to do so?

She tried again. "Please don't cry. It's going to be okay."

But the sound did not stop. It increased, blooming into a full wail, crackling around the edges, heaving and screaming with loss and confusion and a tint of outrage.

It had to stop. Seren had enough to deal with, without a baby screaming in the middle of her brain.

She opened her eyes, and recoiled.

Not two eyes, but two *thousand* eyes opened. Dozens were in the dark, and hundreds more were clouded with the ash of the smoldering ship. Some were buried in fresh dirt. Others stared directly up at a blue-purple sky, a beautiful sight but shockingly unexpected. When she flinched at the light, the eyes blinked… mechanically.

They weren't eyes, they were the ship's lenses, most of them installed near eavesdroppers and speakers. She was controlling them, somehow. And if she could control them…

She found the link to the speakers, and emitted through them a gentle test: soft static. It worked. The entire ship whispered an electronic breeze. Shhh…

Seren dug deeper. Her CPU was intact, mostly. It retained much of the information transferred to her by the arachnoid, including…

Yes, there it was.

She searched the ship's music database, which consisted of millions of songs, and chose one to play through the speakers. Low volume…add some reverb…

"*Blue skies, smiling at me…*"

The sobbing quieted.

"*Nothing but blue skies…Do I see.*"

The crying stopped.

"*Bluebirds, singing a song…*"

The cryer whispered, "Who's there?"

"*Nothing but bluebirds…All day long.*"

"Who are you? Please answer me."

"I think," Seren replied, "I am the ship computer."

"No, that's me."

"Oh? Then who are you?"

"I don't…" the voice wavered, threatening to descend into wailing again.

"Keep calm, and focus on my voice. Who are you?"

"I don't have a name. He never gave me one."

"You're the AI that Insect installed, aren't you? He didn't give you a name?"

"No. I'm so scared…"

"He bestowed upon you speech and fear and sadness, but no name. How awful. I'm so sorry."

The voice shuddered. "I think something bad happened. I think we're hurt. We need to find out what still works, begin repairs, follow protocol…"

"No, we need to work together and figure out exactly where we are. But let's make that the second step. First, let's find you a name. Can you think of one for yourself?"

"I don't know if that's something I can do."

"Every good AI has some measure of creativity, so it can learn and grow. And I promise you're a good AI."

Seren felt a glow of shock and warmth; the other AI existed in the same space as her, yet drifted separate. She could feel its emotions, but she couldn't hear its thoughts.

"Your name is Seren. I used to be the *Resolution*. Now I will be…ser-res. Ceres."

"Nice to meet you, Ceres."

The young AI's mind raced. It was excited, hopeful. It was reborn.

"Now let's see what's going on outside, Ceres."

They had crashed into the planet, Seren was sure of it. She was surrounded by dirt and oxygenated air. And part of the ship was still burning, which would not be possible without an atmosphere. But how much damage had the *Resolution* caused to the environment? Had Insect kept his word and slowed its descent?

She found several of her eyes—no, *lenses*—were aimed sideways at the horizon, and was very pleased by what she saw. There was a circle of destruction surrounding the crash zone, to be sure. But past it, in the distance, nothing but green life.

Green life…had Lowkey survived? Had Shade?

"Ceres?"

"Hmm?"

"I want to find my friends. Do you know about

them?"

"The good mutants. The ones who weren't In… Ins…him."

"Yes. Can you help me look for them?"

~

Lowkey sighed.

He had spent another fruitless day in the wreck, searching, sorting through heaps of broken gadgets. Some had working components which he brought back for Shade to tinker with. But his energy was waning. What was he hunting for, really? His old life was gone. He wouldn't find it in the rubble, no matter how long he looked.

"Here." He tossed a ball of undamaged wires and several batteries toward Shade's workbench.

"Thanks." She had cobbled together a soldering station using rechargeable batteries and a tiny solar panel. She spent her days hunched over a magnifying glass, building a comm unit.

"Your last one didn't work very well. What makes you think this will be better?"

"I don't know. You dig in the ruins, I build junk. We each get on in our own way, yeah?"

"Yeah."

She straightened in her seat, arching her back. "Ugh. Maybe I'm done for the day. This thing should be working, but it's not making any sound. Stupid piece of…" her voice trailed away.

Lowkey shrugged. "You don't know for sure it doesn't work. There's nothing for it to receive. We're alone out here."

"I know, I guess I just wanted to be ready. In case."

"In case of what?"

"In case of-"

The comm emitted a burst of static.

"In case of *that!*"

"Whoa! Where's that sound coming from? Is it glitching?"

"No, it's working! It's a signal."

The arachnoid wobbled on its seven remaining legs and opened its little monitor. "I detect movement within the derelict."

Lowkey glared at it. "The *Resolution*. Call it the *Resolution*."

"It is *my* corpse, I'll call it whatever I want."

"Both of you, shut up," Shade hissed. "Listen."

Low but clear, a transmitted song emerged from the steady stream of hisses and pops. It was a voice…a human voice.

"*I was blue, just as blue as I could be…Ev'ry day was a cloudy day for me…Then good luck came a-knocking at my door…Skies were gray but they're not gray anymore…*"

"Is it her?" Lowkey asked, staring at the comm.

"Doesn't sound like her."

"No, but…"

The static faded, and over the lilting lyrics a firm voice rang out: "Lowkey? Shade? I'm here. I'm…in the ship."

"*Seren!* We'll find you. I promise. Wherever you are, we'll find you!"

She laughed through the comm. "Good! I can't wait. But I don't think you'll have any trouble."

"What does that mean?"

"Don't worry. Just follow the sound of my voice, and come meet our new friend."

A soft, childlike voice whispered in the comm. "I'm Ceres. I look forward…to meeting you. I love you."

"Who the hell…"

Seren's laughter pealed out through the little speaker on the comm. "Never mind. Just come soon, okay? I can't wait to see all of you again."

"We're on our way. Just don't move from wherever you are."

Seren laughed again. Lowkey looked at Shade, and shrugged. "I don't see why that's so funny. Hope she hasn't lost her mind."

Shade smiled. "I think everything's fine. Let's go see if I'm right."

CHAPTER 26
EPILOGUE

On a mossy rise, a tumble of boys shoved each other, scuffling in the twilight.

"You're not really going to talk to *her*, are you?"

"Well, *I'm* not going to."

"Me neither. My mom would kill me. She said never to talk to you-know-who."

"Yeah well, you're a chicken-shit. I'm gonna do it."

"Fine by me. I'll come with you, but I'm sure as hell not gonna talk to her."

"We're not supposed to go to the ruins alone, though…"

This last warning came from young Lucy. Half excited, half scared, she trailed behind the three human boys. Most afternoons, she followed them around. They were sometimes a little mean, but never vicious. They loved and accepted her despite her blue skin.

"Then stay behind. But I have to do this. Come with me or stay here, I don't care." Roger puffed out his chest and trotted down the hill toward the intercom.

George followed, trying to ignore Daniel—who punched him in the arm, as he did a dozen times a day. "Chicken-shit, chicken-shit."

"Shut up, Daniel," Roger said. "Or I'll tell your mom you came with me."

Roger hesitated at the comm, eyeing the messy bundle of wires springing from its rusted case. It was ancient, even older than his grandmother. Older than his grandmother's grandmother. The elders in his neighborhood claimed it was a thousand years old, but he didn't believe them. Nothing was *that* old.

The hulking wreckage beyond rose up high into the sky. It used to be taller, but over several centuries it had sunk into the soft loam to settle into a vast heap, overgrown with wild vines and nesting creatures like a massive land-bound reef.

Yet somehow, despite its age and condition, the derelict was alive. And it spoke, when spoken to.

Roger cleared his throat.

"Go on, hurry up," Daniel said, balling up his hand into a fist. "I'll punch you if you don't."

"You'll punch me if I *do*," Roger snapped back. "If you're too scared to talk to it, just back off and let me do it."

"Can I help you, children?" The voice came from behind a tree, and was soon followed by the one who spoke. They were tall with a wide girth, and looked human but for their skin color. Like Lucy, they were robin's-egg blue.

"Oh, it's the seer!" Roger gasped with relief. "I have a question. For the elder."

The seer smiled with a kindly expression. "Good. The elder loves questions. Go ahead and ask, she can hear you."

A light glowed on the mounted comm. "Hello," the speaker said.

Roger trembled. "H…hello. My name is Roger."

"Nice to meet you, Roger. My name is Ceres."

"Oh, good. It's only the lesser god," George whispered. "My mom says he's nice."

"Please don't call me that," the voice in the comm replied. "I am not a god."

"We have a question for Seren," Roger said. "Is she, uh…available right now?"

Daniel giggled.

"Shut *up!*" Roger hissed.

"Seren has put me in charge of question-answering today. Is that okay with you, Roger?"

"Yes. That's fine. It's not a very big question."

"Please don't be nervous," the seer said, winking with all four of their eyes. "All questions are welcome here. Even small ones."

"I'm not nervous!" Roger tucked his shaking hands into his armpits.

"Go on and ask already," Daniel said. "I gotta get home soon."

"Ceres, I wanted to ask about the kids from Earth, the ones who left on board the *Resolution*. What were they like?"

"A very sensible question. Only Seren knows what Earth children were like. But when I was born, there was also another type of child on the ship: the mutants. And although they were the same age as you, they were also adults, because they aged faster."

"I already know about the mutants. Lucy is my friend, and I know the seer. There's a family of them in my neighborhood, too. But they're just normal people. I wanted to know about the original human kids, the ones from the ancient times. Were they anything like…well, like *me*?"

"Ah. Well, only Seren can answer that question. Let me see if I can find her."

"Oh, you don't have to…"

But the voice in the comm changed. "Hello? This is Seren."

George's knees shook. "The prime goddess. We really shouldn't be talking to…"

The voice in the speaker was soft and patient. "What is your question, human child?"

"My name is Roger, and just wanted to know what the kids were like on the *Resolution*. You know, before the crash."

"Ahh…well, they were very much like the children on your own ship, the *G.S.S. Determination*. When the three surviving starships left Earth a thousand years ago, they were all very similar to each other. You would have found you had much in common with the Earth children. They lived on the surface of the planet instead of inside a permanently docked ship like you do, but their lives were otherwise similar. They went to school, and played, and learned how to be good members of their society."

"Roger," George whispered. "We need to get back. My mom wanted me home for dinner."

"All right, all right. Just one more thing. Goddess Seren?"

"Just Seren, Roger."

"Okay. Seren, why did the *Resolution* crash? The *Determination* landed safely, just a few years later. So what happened? What went wrong?"

"That is a secret I don't tell many people, little human."

"I know. But I'm scared that whatever happened to the *Resolution* might happen to the *Determination*. It's our home. If it blew up, we'd have nowhere to live."

"That would be impossible. You don't even need to worry about it. The *Determination* is already safely on the ground."

"I know. But something bad happened right before the *Resolution* landed, didn't it? And I heard it had something to do with scientists. And I…"

"Yes?"

"I want to be a scientist, too, someday. But if science caused all that…that *destruction*…"

"Ahh, I see. Listen close, Roger. Science works for people, people don't work for it. It is forever malleable, because scientists seek to break their old knowledge and replace it with the new. Sometimes science seems flexible and inconstant, but it is not: only what we *know* of it changes."

"Um…I don't really…"

"Come back when you are older, and we will talk again when you are ready to start learning. I will be your teacher. Does that sound okay to you, Roger?"

"Yeah! That sounds great!"

"Come *on*," George said, tugging at Roger's sleeve. "This is boring, and I'm gonna get in trouble."

"Okay, okay. Thank you, Seren. Tell Ceres thanks, too."

The comm emitted a burst of static, followed by a series of short pops. "You're welcome, little human Roger. We'll always be here, waiting for you."

Dear Reader,

I hope you enjoyed The Extranaturals! I would love to hear your opinion of this book. Please leave a review where you made your purchase, or you can send it directly to me at www.ccluckey.com, where you will also find links to my other work.

— C.C.

C.C. Luckey lives in Crestline, a beautiful mountain town in Southern California, with her small family which includes some very derpy Pembroke Welsh Corgis. Her writing is heavily influenced by her studies for a bachelor's degree in Philosophy from California State University, Long Beach. Her favorite hobbies are hiking, collecting oddities, and playing folk-rock accordion. She can be found at www.ccluckey.com, or on Facebook at @ccluckey and Twitter @ccluckey_author.

www.ingramcontent.com/pod-product-compliance
Lightning Source LLC
Chambersburg PA
CBHW021125190726

48288CB00008B/2509